CALCULATED DESTRUCTION

Blade spoke to the huddled, frightened crowd. "This is a machine of the Sky Masters, made for war. It has gone mad with age. Saorm and I will attempt to lead the robot away from here and destroy it."

Without wasting another moment Blade and Saorm darted into the street where the robot was still standing. They opened fire. Instantly the robot turned its head, its body followed the head with surprising speed, and the laser chewed a piece out of a wall above the two men. A fragment large enough to crush Blade's skull missed him by a fraction of an inch.

"To the right!" Saorm followed Blade's gesture and ducked into a side street. The robot fired again, totally demolishing two buildings, leaving the street a pile of smoking rubble. Sheltered for the moment in a doorway, Blade desperately hoped the creature would fall victim to the falling masonry. But the robot was sensitive to danger and avoided the crashing stone, continuing its advance on the two men, undeterred.

Blade knew nothing could be accomplished by running. But what could two men do against a war machine armed with lasers?

THE BLADE SERIES:

BLADE

THE RUINS OF KALDAC
Jeffrey Lord

PINNACLE BOOKS   NEW YORK

BLADE #34: THE RUINS OF KALDAK

Copyright © 1981 by Book Creations, Inc.

An original Pinnacle Books edition, published for the first time anywhere.

Produced by Book Creations, Inc.
Executive Producer: Lyle Kenyon Engel

First printing, July 1981

ISBN: 0-523-41208-8

Printed in the United States of America

PINNACLE BOOKS, INC.
1430 Broadway
New York, New York 10018

The Ruins of Kaldak

Chapter 1

The sky was gray, and a chilly wind blew rain through empty windows, turning the dust on the floor into mud. The tall man standing by the doorway looked out briefly at the foul weather, then shrugged and walked back into the room.

The man was not only tall. He was also heavily built, with a broad chest and muscle-corded arms and legs to match. He still moved with a light step which hinted at speed and coordination as well as sheer muscle. His hair was black, and his skin was deeply tanned under the dirt. His skin also showed marks and ridges which could only be the scars of painful wounds. He was naked except for a loinguard which gleamed in the dim light with a silvery metallic sheen, but in spite of the breeze he was not shivering.

The man's name was Richard Blade. He was probably the only man in any world who'd traveled into more than thirty different Dimensions, fought deadly battles in all of them, and always returned alive.

Richard Blade didn't worry anymore about whether each Dimension he visited could really be called a complete "world." One Dimension certainly reached out many light-years to the stars, but that didn't mean they all did. In some Dimensions he'd never seen more than an area smaller than his native England. Neither made much difference to his chances of coming back alive. After a while he left the question of the Dimension's size more and more to Lord Leighton, the scientist who'd opened the road to new Dimensions. As long as he came back in one piece, Richard Blade, who was essentially a practical man, was content. Before he started traveling among the Dimensions, he was a field operative for the secret British intelligence agency MI6A.

Lord Leighton was quite a different proposition. Before he discovered the road to new Dimensions, he'd already had a long career as one of Britain's most brilliant scientists. He was born a hunchback, and polio twisted his legs when he was a child, but there was nothing wrong with his mind. Even his best friends would admit that there was a great deal wrong with his manners, which were abominable, but even his worst enemies would admit that his mind was a precision instrument of extraordinary brilliance.

Leighton had developed a theory that if the mind of a physically robust and highly intelligent man was linked to a powerful computer, a new form of intelligence would emerge. He chose Richard Blade, linked him to a computer of his own invention, and wound up sending Richard Blade off into an unknown world.

The discovery of what they called "Dimension X" was a complete accident, but that didn't make it any less important. There had to be untapped natural resources and new scientific discoveries waiting out there in Dimension X. If they could just be brought home to Britain, then put to use. . . .

Several years and several million pounds later, Project Dimension X was only a little ahead of where it started. Richard Blade was still the only man who could travel into Dimension X and return alive. He still couldn't return to a particular Dimension except by accident. He still couldn't take much equipment with him or bring back anything except by chance. Some of what he brought back was no more than exotic junk. Some of it was jewels or precious metals which could at least be sold to raise money for the Project. Some of it was knowledge or technology which would be priceless when and if it could be put to practical use.

However, things seemed to be looking up a trifle. Blade paced around the gloomy room and listened to the rain, fingering the belt of his silvery loinguard. That was something based on Dimension X technology, and he'd worn it safely through the transition into this Dimension!

Blade thought of the first time he'd seen the loinguard, just this morning. He'd arrived at the Tower of London a few minutes early, then waited under the hard eyes of the Special Branch men who guarded the entrance to the Project. Eventually J arrived, as erect and ageless as ever, looking like a retired civil servant rather than one of the great spymasters of modern times. He'd chosen Blade straight out of Oxford for MI6A. He still headed the agency, but now he was also chief of security for Project Dimension X. He was about the best qualified man for the job, and it also let him keep a watchful eye out for Blade, who was the closest thing to a son he'd ever known.

The two men rode down in the elevator to the Project's complex buried two hundred feet underground. Then they took the walk down the long gleaming corridor to the computer rooms. By now Blade could have walked the corridor blindfolded. As they passed the last of the electronic sentinels which monitored the corridor for intruders, J turned to Blade. "Leighton called me last night, Blade. Said he's got a surprise for us."

Blade managed to restrain his enthusiasm. A "surprise" from Lord Leighton could be almost anything. It was likely to be a new development the scientist thought he or J would oppose if they knew about it too far in advance. Lord Leighton's creativity and enthusiasm sometimes ran ahead of his good judgment.

"Did he say anything else?"

J nodded. "He said it had to do with the Englor Alloy #2."

That was somewhat more encouraging. In one Dimension Blade found a country called Englor, strangely like Home Dimension England in many ways, locked in a deadly struggle with an opponent just as strangely like the Soviet Union. Englor's airplanes were built of alloys far beyond anything in Home Dimension, and Blade brought back formulas and samples for several of them.

It turned out that the most powerful electrical field imaginable would flow through an object made of Alloy #2 from Englor as if it weren't there. When Blade traveled into Dimension X, he was surrounded by a strong electrical field and couldn't wear anything which might disrupt its flow. With equipment made of Alloy #2, he might hope to reach Dimension X in something more than his bare skin, armed with something more than his bare hands!

Unfortunately there were problems in producing Englor Alloy #2 (EA 2 for short) with Home Dimension technology. The problems had been solved only to the point where a few ounces could be produced each day, at a cost of more than five pounds an ounce. On his last trip into Dimension X, Blade carried a length of wire made of EA 2. It made the round trip with him, so at least the theory about traveling with the alloy was sound enough. Now it seemed that Lord Leighton might have some practical applications of the theory to show Blade and J.

Leighton met them at the entrance to the computer rooms and scuttled ahead of them to his private workshop. He looked rather like a gnome hurrying to show his treasure. The surprise lay on the wooden table in the workshop. Blade picked it up and turned it over several times in his hands. It was a loinguard shaped exactly like a standard athletic supporter but made entirely of EA 2. Blade would have recognized the silvery sheen, the flexibility, and the light weight even if J hadn't informed him.

Blade put the loinguard back on the table and looked at the scientist. "Thank you for the thought, sir. But I'm not one of those people who keep their brains between their legs."

A choking sound made Blade turn around. He saw J trying to stifle laughter. To give the older man time to recover, Blade turned back to Leighton. "Joking aside, sir, why this particular piece of equipment?"

"Two reasons," said Leighton. "One, it was the biggest thing we could make with the amount of EA 2 we had and still have enough left over for further experiments. We *could* have made you a small helmet, but we'd have had nothing left except your wire and some scraps and powder."

"I see."

"Two, you've often carped about arriving in other dimensions stark naked. Well, now you have something to

4

wear—an immodest garment, to be sure—nevertheless, it does cover you somewhat, and it *does* protect a vulnerable part of your body. You wouldn't deny that, would you?"

Blade laughed. "Hardly." An injury there could easily cripple a man from pain or loss of blood, even if it didn't castrate him, so maybe the silver loinguard did have *some* practical use. It was reassuring for Blade to realize that even if Lord Leighton sometimes acted like a mad scientist, he still had Blade's best interests in mind. Blade remembered the splitting headaches he used to have when he woke up in Dimension X, before Leighton invented the KALI capsule. Sometimes those headaches were so bad he wouldn't have found it easy to either fight or run. The KALI capsule got rid of them, which improved his chances for survival.

But now Blade's mouth tightened as he remembered all the people the KALI capsule *hadn't* helped to survive. Leighton had the seven-foot capsule controlled by a new, self-programming computer. The computer opened a path between the Dimensions to a monstrosity called the Ngaa. It killed more than thirty people, put the whole world in danger, and nearly destroyed Project Dimension X before Blade fought and destroyed it in one of his grimmest battles.

One of the Ngaa's victims was Zoé Cornwall, once Blade's fiancée. He now knew that he was never likely to love another woman the same way, yet he would never be able to marry a woman he didn't love as he'd loved Zoé. Considering how he made his living, that was probably just as well, at least for the woman.

Still, Zoé should not have been dead! Blade had not allowed himself to grow bitter and no longer held her death against Lord Leighton. He also did not let himself forget her. He had to remember that Lord Leighton's scientific genius was something like a two-edged sword, which could slash both friends and enemies.

Blade picked up the loinguard again. "Can I get this off in a hurry if I have to?"

"Yes." Leighton pointed. "See—there's a quick-release hook on the side."

Blade saw the hook but tested it several times before he

5

put the loinguard back on the table. He still wasn't entirely sure this wasn't a bawdy joke by Lord Leighton, but it was also a step on the way to arriving better-equipped—and better "dressed"—in Dimension X. That meant survival.

"I'll take a chance," he said. "What do you think, sir?" he asked J.

J frowned. "Well, Richard, it's your—ah, *anatomy*."

"And I might add, Richard," Leighton now said, "your traveling to and from Dimension X with this garment brings us one step closer to making an alloy-wire weapon or even an alloy-wire suit that will increase not only your survival chances but also those of another traveler to Dimension X. Assuming you and the alloy return intact, and once we produce enough of the alloy in our laboratories, we can attempt to send someone else with you to Dimension X. You'd like a companion, wouldn't you, Richard?"

Blade shrugged, but he well knew that the Project's success would be greatly enhanced if someone else could be sent to Dimension X. That other person, lacking Blade's genius for survival, would need a special weapon or the alloy-wire suit for protection. And, yes, Blade thought, he would enjoy having a companion from home in Dimension X.

When Blade climbed into the seven-foot KALI capsule an hour later, he was wearing the silver loinguard. He also wore the usual coat of black grease to guard against electrical burns. He wasn't exactly nervous, but anyone watching him would have noticed how carefully and thickly he greased his penis and groin.

He lay down in the capsule and the lid closed over him, to leave him in the familiar coffinlike darkness with the lining of the capsule pressing against him everywhere. He felt the loinguard staying snugly in place. Good. It wouldn't make any difference at this end if it slipped out of position, but at the other end it might snag on something. That could be embarrassing.

Then the world around Blade dissolved in light and the KALI capsule seemed to vanish. The computer room with the looming crackle-finished consoles was all around him, with Leighton at the master control panel and J in the folding observer seat. He could see everything clearly, but it had all turned a hundred shades of blue. Leighton's white hair was an electric blue, the gray consoles were midnight blue, the red master switch was the color of a robin's egg—

For a moment uncertainty caught Blade by the throat. The KALI capsule had never put him through one of these psychedelic displays before. Was the loinguard affecting the electrical field around him after all?

Then the blue laboratory exploded into a hundred shapeless pieces, each a different shade of blue. A high-pitched whine like an enormous mosquito tore at Blade's ears. Then there was only blackness for a moment, and after that damp grass under his back and a chilly wind blowing across his skin. . . .

Now Blade continued to pace around the desolate room listening to the relentless sound of the rain. He felt as if he was the only man in all of Dimension X.

Chapter 2

Blade had found the room after a short search. When he first arrived in Dimension X he had discovered that he was sitting halfway up a steep hill covered with long grass. He felt no trace of a headache. He stood up, stretched his arms and legs, then unhooked his loinguard and examined it. Both the loinguard and what it was intended to protect seemed to be intact. As he put the loinguard back on, a stronger gust of wind made the grass around him dance wildly. Then thunder rumbled across the hillside and the gray skies overhead let loose with a downpour of cold rain.

Blade had looked hastily around for shelter. Visibility was shrinking rapidly, so it was hard to make out details.

As far as he could tell, there were ruins at the bottom of the hill. He saw what looked like walls with gaping windows, a tower reduced to a jagged fang, a rubble-choked street lined with trees tossing their branches in the storm, but nothing which promised protection from the weather. He turned and looked uphill.

On the crest of the hill stood a grayish block which looked like an unruined building. He watched for a moment, looking for any signs of life, saw none, then started cautiously up the hill. He would have liked to run up to the nearest door and get out of the rain, but the building was the most conspicuous object and probably the best shelter for miles around. Others in the area might also have their eyes on it, and he didn't plan to walk into an ambush, so he proceeded slowly.

Blade stopped every few yards, noticing new details about the building each time. He saw that one side of it was dark except for some blurred white shapes on the wall near the ground. He saw that one wing had nearly collapsed. Moss grew on some of the leaning slabs, while creepers grew up the cracked walls and over the tiles of the roof.

At last he reached the hilltop and walked completely around the building. He suddenly realized that the blurred white shapes on the darkened wall were the silhouettes of human beings, distorted by many years of weathering. Blade had seen something similar—in photographs taken at Hiroshima and Nagasaki. When the atomic bomb had exploded there, the flash darkened the walls of buildings everywhere except where people had been standing close by. The victims' bodies left white shadows on the walls, just like these shadows Blade saw now. So there had been an atomic bomb explosion in this Dimension, Blade realized.

For a moment Blade considered moving on, to avoid any possible danger from lingering radiation. Then he realized that the darkened wall still showed traces of the bomb only because it was on the side of the building away from the prevailing winds. On the other side the walls were undarkened, and grass and plants were growing. Certainly enough time had passed for the building to be free of any dangerous radioactivity. Blade tore a branch from a bush

8

growing by the door and made an improvised club, then strode into the building.

It was as deserted inside as it was outside, except for a few small skittering shapes which immediately vanished into the walls. They were about the size of mice but didn't move like them. Blade thought of radiation-induced mutations.

In one room he had found blurred footprints, but they were in ankle-deep dust. Whoever made the footprints had come and gone years ago. Blade found he had the choice of four rooms which were reasonably dry except for the rain blowing in through the windows. He'd picked the one with the least dust, and now he finally stopped pacing and thinking about all the incidents leading up to his arrival in Dimension X. He decided he needed to get some sleep, and he curled up in the corner farthest from the door but closest to the window. After a moment he sat up, unhooked his loinguard, and wrapped it around his left hand. The club and the loinguard were the best weapons he could hope for tonight, and the metal wire was getting cold against his bare skin.

Blade curled up again and started willing himself to go to sleep, in spite of the damp chill. He hoped Lord Leighton's plans to provide him with more survival equipment succeeded, and quickly. Right now he would have given a good deal for a down sleeping bag or even a blanket and thick pile of dry leaves!

By morning the wind had died and the rain was only a drizzle, although the sky was still a depressing gray. A few minutes of vigorous exercises got Blade's blood flowing again. By the time he'd finished exercising, the clouds were beginning to break up. Visibility rapidly increased to several miles. That was enough to tell Blade that there were probably no friends or enemies anywhere close enough to matter.

At the foot of the hill Blade saw a ruined city, hundreds of crumbling buildings along rubble-choked streets radiating out from a central tower. Beyond the city lay a solid wall of dark green forest. Beyond that Blade saw a line of what could have been either oddly-shaped hills or truly gigantic buildings. At this distance and with clouds still lying low on the horizon, he couldn't be sure.

Everything seemed weirdly lifeless. The city was half-overgrown with bushes and trees, and the forest beyond looked as dense as a jungle. Blade saw no tracks on the ground, no birds in the air. He couldn't hear any birds or insects even when he held his breath to listen, nothing but the sigh and moan of the wind. After a while this eerie silence drove him into action. He hurried around to the other side of the building and looked west.

On this side the hill sloped away more gently, leveling out in an immense grassy plain. The plain began less than half a mile away and continued all the way to the horizon, as flat and featureless as a billiard table. Far off to the north Blade saw what looked like one end of an enormous bridge, with more ruined buildings clustered around it. He couldn't see what the bridge crossed, or any more signs of life than he'd seen elsewhere.

Blade tore off another branch and started tying it with lengths of vine to the first branch, to make a heavier club. By the time he'd finished, his hands were red and sore from the acid sap of the creepers. He'd also decided to go east, exploring the ruined city at the foot of the hill, then cutting through the forest. What lay on the far side of the forest certainly looked more interesting than the plain to the west. The forest would also give him better shelter from the weather and probably more food. He took a last look around the ruined building, then started down the hill.

It didn't take Blade long to see all of the ruined city he needed to see. One rubble-clogged street or one house with its windows and doors gaping like the eye sockets of a skull looked very much like another. Like the building on the hill, the city had been abandoned for generations, possibly centuries. Unlike the building, it had been visited a number of times after its people abandoned it. Blade saw ragged holes in a dozen walls, where fixtures had been pulled or chopped free. He saw rooms swept almost clean of dust. Under an overhanging piece of roof he found the remains of a campfire and a pile of animal droppings no more than a few weeks old. Blade looked briefly for the animals'

10

tracks, then realized the night's rain would have completely wiped them out.

The visitors seldom went above the third floor and apparently never went into the cellars. Blade struggled down some of the crumbling, treacherous flights of stairs and found whole untouched piles of metal waiting for him. Much of it was so rusted or corroded he couldn't tell what it had been, but he found a piece with a sharp point just the right size to be used one-handed. He also found strips of a plasticlike material which he wrapped around one end of the piece of metal to give him a better grip on this improvised knife. A longer strip of the plastic tied around his waist made a belt.

Blade came up from the last cellar faster than he'd gone down. It was definitely inhabited—by ordinary-looking mice and by something considerably larger which never left the shadows in a corner. Blade could only hear its chittering and the scrabbling of claws, on stone, and smell an unbelievably rank odor.

By the time Blade left the city the clouds were almost gone, and it was a bright, if somewhat chilly, day. He could now see clearly that the tall shapes beyond the forest to the east were colossal buildings. They stood so close together that some of them were linked by aerial bridges, and most of them looked nearly intact. Blade was sure that their appearance was deceptive, but the towers would provide better shelter than the ruins. They should also tell him more about the fate of this Dimension and its people.

The moment Blade plunged into the forest, he was back in twilight. The trees grew in such regular order that it was clear they'd been planted that way. No doubt the spaces between the trees were wide enough when the park was laid out. Now, after long years of neglect, the ground between the trees was overgrown with bushes, ferns, and vines. Blade lost a good deal of skin pushing through some particularly thick patches. He kept going, since he didn't want to spend the night in the forest or reach the city after dark if he could help it.

Around mid-afternoon he came out onto the bank of a sluggish, weed-choked stream, with an unmistakable path on the far bank. He probed the stream with a fallen branch

11

and learned he'd be swimming rather than wading across it. He was about to slip into the water when a patch of the weeds started swirling back and forth. Then a long row of black bony spines broke the surface briefly, heading toward Blade. He pulled his foot out of the water just as the creature swam close enough to give him a good look at it.

It looked like a cross between a giant catfish, a piranha, and a stingray. It had spines on either side of its jaws as well as along its back, a large mouth full of needle-sharp teeth, and a long thin tail with a barb on the end. It was at least nine feet long and coal-black except for sickly green eyes.

Blade decided that swimming across the stream might not be such a good idea after all. He started working his way upstream, looking for bridges or fallen trees. He found neither, but eventually he came to the ruins of a small dam. Beyond the dam the stream spread out in a small lake, but over the top of the dam the water was no more than ankle-deep. Blade crossed the top of the dam as fast as he dared go on the crumbling, slimy stones, keeping a watchful eye on the lake. Two sets of black spines rose near the dam only moments after he reached dry land and the path.

Once on the path he moved more easily but also more cautiously. The existence of a path implied the existence of someone to make it, and Blade didn't want to surprise or be surprised by that someone.

So he moved from one patch of cover to the next, looking and listening around him before each move. The path was obviously in fairly regular use, but there'd been too much rain last night even here under the trees to leave any footprints.

Roughly a mile down the path from the stream, Blade stopped abruptly. On either side of the path, ferns, vines, bushes, and even small trees were crushed into the ground. A trail of more of the same damage led off into the woods to the left. A large tree at the head of the trail showed a black scar. Blade looked more closely at the tree. Something had gouged out bark and wood to a depth of at least six inches, and also burned the edges of the wound to char-coal.

Blade followed the trail. It came to an end within fifty yards, and the smell stopped Blade even sooner. Decay and insects hadn't left enough of the animal to make it worth going closer. It must have been about the size of a large bear, and its skull and ribs showed the same sort of blackening as the tree.

Blade began to wonder just how primitive the people of this Dimension were. They'd obviously wrecked much of their civilization. Just as obviously, they had enough technology left to produce a weapon very much like a laser. That didn't make them any less dangerous, of course. Civilized people can be as unfriendly to strangers as primitive ones. With machine guns, lasers, and artillery they can also be unfriendly at a much greater range and in a much more destructive way.

It was also more important than before to get out of the woods before nightfall. Blade was sure he could outtalk, outfight, or if necessary outrun most human opponents. He wasn't nearly so confident he could do the same with a creature ten times his weight and probably carnivorous.

Blade returned to the path and started off again, moving a good deal more briskly than before.

Chapter 3

Blade covered at least two miles at a trot, then saw the path was sloping downhill. At the same time the trees began to thin out. Soon Blade could make out the tumbled, overgrown stone blocks of a wall ahead. He climbed over the wall and picked his way across another stream on the half-submerged ruins of a bridge. After a few hundred yards more through young trees, Blade found himself on an open hillside. The sun was still well above the horizon.

At the foot of the hill the city of towers loomed against a pale sky. In the clear air Blade felt he could reach out and touch it. Even from this distance it showed remarkably little damage. Most of the windows and doors were black and gaping, and here and there stone had crumbled or metal paneling had corroded through. Bushes sprouted from cracks in the streets, and the wreckage of one of the aerial bridges completely blocked an intersection. Otherwise the city might have been sleeping rather than dead. It was easy to tell that its builders had loved beauty and put that love into their city, without a thought for the war which their love of beauty hadn't been able to prevent.

On the hillside sloping down to the city, Blade saw clusters of ruined buildings. Some of the clusters were practically small towns in themselves, others were isolated and overgrown. The "suburbs" hadn't been so robustly built as the towers of the city itself.

In a way, Blade found the city of towers a more depressing sight than the ruins to the west. He was glad it was late enough in the day to give him an excuse to stay out of the city until morning. He didn't care for the thought of prowling dark streets where the least superstitious man might find himself watching and listening for ghosts.

Blade stiffened as he realized the morbid and dangerous turn his thoughts were taking. He'd been letting his attention wander, at a time when he had to be even more alert than he'd been in the forest. He took cover behind a bush and found that when he could no longer see those dead towers looming over him, the gloomy thoughts went away.

He also realized that if he hadn't been alone he wouldn't have felt this way. He wouldn't be too particular about the company, either. He remembered some of his old comrades from MI6A, dour men who seldom talked about anything except their profession and the price of whisky. Even one of them would have been a relief.

Blade was as much a loner as any sane man can be. He wouldn't have joined MI6A in the first place if he wasn't. But even a man as naturally solitary as a cat can occasionally want someone to talk to or at least to guard his back. But Blade didn't even have someone else who'd faced the

14

dangers of Dimension X and could swap stories with him over a bottle of Scotch! According to Leighton, they were one step closer to sending someone else to Dimension X, once an alloy-weapon or suit could be manufactured to increase the survival chances. Still, even if such a protective device were made, they'd still have to find someone who could travel into Dimension X and return alive and sane, and the search for such a person was as far from success as ever.

Blade decided that if he had a choice between a happy marriage in Home Dimension and a comrade-in-arms for travel into Dimension X, he'd choose the second. It was hard to imagine a woman worth marrying who would accept being shut out of most of her husband's working life. She would be shut out—the Official Secrets Act would see to that. Even worse, she'd have a good chance of ending up a widow without ever being allowed to know how!

Blade rose, stepped out into the open, then stopped in midstride. Smoke and dust were rising from one of the clusters of ruins, less than half a mile away. Then he saw running figures burst out of the ruins onto the open hillside. They seemed to be human, with dark skins or wearing dark clothing. Some ran singly, others in pairs. Darker shapes, low to the ground, seemed to be running after the people and among them. As Blade watched he saw the reddish flicker of sunset light on metal, then a longer, greenish glow which looked artificial. Lasers?

Blade drew his knife and started down the hill, using every bit of cover he could. About halfway down the hill he saw what the low dark shapes were. He saw the short legs, the smooth brown coats, the pointed heads with ugly red eyes, the obscenely hairless tails.

Rats.

Rats the size of German Shepherds!

Blade charged out from behind a stretch of broken wall and plunged down the hill like an Olympic sprinter.

Blade loathed rats. He'd loathed them ever since a night on one of his first missions for MI6A. He'd spent that night in a hut on the outskirts of Calcutta, along with the rat-gnawed corpse of a baby no more than three months

15

old. Ever since that night he'd killed rats any time he had a chance, coolly, efficiently, and as thoroughly as possible.

Blade went down the hill with all thoughts of having no one to guard his back quite forgotten. He didn't quite forget that he had a back to guard. He never went that far, one of the reasons he was still alive after so many years of enough dangers to kill a dozen men. Instead of staying under cover of the ruins, Blade now stayed in the open, as far from any cover as possible. Crumbling walls and fallen roofs could hide the rats. With his knife and club, Blade could fight them safely only if he saw them coming a long way off. It would also help if he didn't suddenly burst out of nowhere at the people fighting the rats. They might be just a little bit trigger-happy right now!

Blade counted about a dozen people and at least twice that many rats. Four of the people seemed to be armed with rifles firing lasers or some other type of energy beam. The others carried bows or spears. All of them carried short swords strapped to their hips. So far none of the rats were close enough to make the people draw their swords.

The battle was moving uphill toward Blade, and the people were leaving a trail of dead or dying rats behind them as they climbed. Every time one rat went down, two or three more seemed to pop out of the ruins, and they were tough. Blade saw one lose a leg to a laser beam but keep coming on three legs until someone else put an arrow through its brain.

Most of the people were dressed in dark leather boots, trousers, and baggy shirts. Some also wore heavy jackets studded with bits of metal, as a crude sort of armor. Blade saw one with both a jacket and a rifle run up the hill toward him, then stop suddenly and turn without noticing the Englishman. A moment later Blade himself had to stop. At his feet was a steep-sided ditch at least ten feet deep and half again as wide, the bottom overgrown with bushes and grass. The angle of the slope had hidden the ditch from Blade.

Now Blade could see that the rifleman was a boy no more than seventeen years old, with long blue-tinged hair caught up in a pigtail and a red sash around his waist. He was kneeling and firing at the oncoming rats with more

16

enthusiasm than accuracy. Blade winced as he saw one laser beam crisp grass at the feet of one of the boy's comrades.

Then suddenly the grass and bushes at the bottom of the ditch churned, and four of the rats scrambled up the side toward the boy. "Behind you!" Blade shouted. The boy whirled, finger closing on the trigger of his rifle. Blade dove for the ground as a laser beam singed his hair. Then the first of the rats reached the boy. He drew his sword, but not before the rat was too close for him to hold it off. Its jaws closed on his leg, and Blade knew from his yell that the leather wasn't tough enough to keep out those yellow-white teeth. The boy hacked down with the sword, splitting the rat's skull but dropping his rifle. It hit the lip of the ditch, teetered, then rolled down a few feet to fetch up against a bush.

Before the rifle stopped rolling, Blade was gathering himself for a leap. As it stopped, he jumped. He landed on hands and knees close to the rifle but closer to one of the rats. It lunged at him. Blade crouched and met it with knife in one hand and the other hand outstretched to guard. He saw that these giant rats moved more slowly in proportion to their size than normal rats.

As the rat closed, Blade's free hand shot forward, closing on the rat's ears. He jerked its head back and his knife slashed, laying the rat's throat open. Then he picked it up one-handed, threw it at its two remaining comrades, and bent down to scoop up the laser rifle.

It looked so simple that Blade couldn't believe anyone could miss with it. Then he missed two shots himself, and one rat got so close that he had to reverse the rifle and crush the rat's skull with the butt. After that he realized he'd been using the laser like a normal bullet-firing weapon, leading his target and allowing for the wind. Laser beams moved at the speed of light, unaffected by wind.

Blade killed the last of the four rats in the ditch with a long blast which nearly tore it in two. It rolled down the slope, its charred guts trailing, to land almost on top of five more rats coming out of the same burrow. They milled around long enough for Blade to drop two of them with shots to the head. He killed a third as it scrambled upward,

17

and burned the tail off a fourth. That slowed it down enough for the boy to kill it with a sword thrust between the eyes. The fifth rat reared up on its hind legs to attack the boy's throat. The boy thrust it through the stomach, its jaws closed on empty air inches short of his throat, and then Blade burned halfway through its neck with his laser.

More rats were scurrying out of their burrow in the ditch as the last corpse rolled down. Blade scrambled up to join the boy on the edge before any of the new rats could start climbing up. The boy took one long look at Blade, examining him from head to foot. Then he shrugged and after that seemed to find nothing unusual about fighting side by side with a nearly naked man half again his size and much lighter-skinned.

Blade picked off rats at long range, and the boy used his sword on any which got close. His wounded leg was bleeding freely, but the wounds didn't seem deep enough to slow him down. They were both too busy killing rats in the ditch to pay attention to the battle behind them. Blade's world shrank down to the matted, blood-smeared grass in the ditch, the blood-spattered boy beside him, the hot rifle in his hands, and the steadily more overpowering smell of burned rat flesh.

Eventually Blade's laser ran out of power in the middle of a burst. The rat was still alive, and the boy jumped down to kill it with his sword. He slipped on the grass and tumbled head over heels to the bottom of the ditch. Blade threw down his useless rifle and got ready to finish off the rat with his knife.

Then a laser beam sizzled past Blade's ankles, and the rat's head exploded gruesomely. He turned around, raising his knife. The man standing there was nearly his own size, with bare arms corded with muscles and covered with scars. His head was shaved bald, and he wore a mustache with small silver beads tied to each end. Wide golden eyes met Blade's for a moment, then shifted their gaze down into the ditch.

"Ho, Bairam!" the man shouted. "Your thoughts are still faster than your eye or your hand. Does nothing change?"

Young Bairam glared at the man in silence for a moment, then pointed at Blade. "Yes it does, Hota. It was this

18

one who saved me, not you. Also he, unlike you, did not use Oltec when the battle was over and death-danger past."

"The death-danger was *not* past. There were still living rats close."

"I saw none."

"You had your eyes turned the wrong way, as usual."

"I had my eyes on these," he said, pointing at the dead or dying rats littering the bottom of the ditch. "And he—" pointing at Blade "—and I kept them from biting you in the ass, until they were all dead. It was then that you used the Oltec. The Law says—"

"You are so sure that you know what the Law says, because you are Peython's son! I have better reason to know what the Law says. I have obeyed it in more battles than you have years."

"Oh? I didn't know you'd fought that many women."

The big man began reciting a list of his battles which Blade found almost impossible to understand. It wasn't the language itself which confused him. The transition into Dimension X had altered the structure of his brain so that he could both speak and understand the local language as if it were English. Why this happened was still a mystery, but Blade didn't mind the alteration going unexplained as long as it didn't stop happening!

The problem with this conversation was that Blade didn't know what two-thirds of the words used meant. "Oltec," for example. Blade thought he remembered a tribe of Central American Indians by that name but seriously doubted he'd landed in Central America! Then "Kaldak," "munfan," and dozens of others. For all the sense he could make of it, the conversation might as well have been taking place in a language he didn't understand.

The quarrel between Bairam and Hota came to an abrupt end when a high-pitched, very cold voice spoke from behind Blade.

"Be quiet, both of you."

Blade helped the boy out of the ditch, then turned to face the speaker. He saw a blue-haired young woman with a laser rifle slung across her chest and a short sword in one hand. Her face was dirty and too thin for real beauty, but her eyes were a glorious deep green with flecks of silver.

19

An armored jacket concealed her above the waist, but one leg of her trousers was ripped open to above the knee. The leg exposed had a magnificent tan which didn't come from a bottle and lovely curves which came from firm muscles instead of support hose.

Right now she sounded too angry to encourage Blade to think how she might look undressed. "I am going to speak to my father about both of you if there is another quarrel like this. Each of you is both right and wrong. Bairam, there were live rats up here, which you could not see. So Hota did not break the Law of Oltec. Hota, you should have let either Bairam or this one have the kill. You were greedy, then you kept the quarrel going after my brother spoke wrongly. You also showed bad sense, in keeping the quarrel alive with *this* one standing close." She turned to Blade, brushing hair out of her eyes and looking hard at him. "Who are you, pale man?"

"He saved my life, Kareena," said Bairam. "Why do you speak to him that way?"

Kareena glared at her brother again. "I know who *you* are." Then she smiled, making her thin face almost beautiful for a moment, and punched her brother lightly in the shoulder. "I know who you are and what you are. I do not know anything about this man."

"I am Richard Blade of England, a land beyond the ocean."

"What ocean?" said Kareena abruptly. The point of her sword hovered within inches of Blade's bare stomach.

"You have not heard of the Gray Ocean?" said Blade, trying to look surprised as he improvised his story. "Then I have come even farther than I imagined. When I fled after killing seven men to avenge my sister's honor, I knew I would have to go far. I did not know I would come to a land where they did not know of the Ocean."

"Your sister must have been a poor creature, if she could not avenge her own honor," said Kareena. But the sword point wavered.

"Against seven men?" said Bairam. "Kareena, be serious. Even you would find those odds too much!"

"You're an odd one to tell me about—" Kareena began sharply, then caught herself as she realized she was about to start another quarrel in front of the stranger. She shrugged, then smiled politely at Blade. "Certainly you are not from Kaldak. From your pale skin I would say you are from no city in all the Land. The Sky Masters were said to have skins like yours, but they are all dead. So your story will be interesting, even if it is not as you have told it. Also, you did save Bairam. That puts me in your debt under the Law, and also our father Peython.

"However, you are not yet within the Law and cannot be until we return to Kaldak. Therefore you cannot bear an Oltec weapon. Will a sword or a spear satisfy your honor as a warrior of England?"

From that, Blade concluded that "Oltec weapon" must mean one of the laser rifles. He really would have preferred to carry one of them, but the rifles were probably rare. Certainly one of them wouldn't save him if these people turned violently hostile. He could help keep them friendly by following their customs.

Ceremoniously Blade picked up his empty laser rifle and handed it to Kareena. "A sword or a spear is enough. I have seen many lands, lived with many peoples, and obeyed the Law of each one. That is honor and also wisdom."

Bairam smiled. "Kareena, how can you doubt a man who speaks such words?"

"Because they are no more than words," said Hota bluntly. "When we know if they are more—" He would have probably started another quarrel, but Kareena was looking ready to strangle both Hota and her brother with her bare hands. She laid the rifle down and turned.

"Sidas! Bring a spear for the pale man Blade. Then everybody be ready to move. There will be no camping here tonight!"

That got a murmur of agreement from the rest of the band, who'd finished off the wounded rats and gathered along the edge of the ditch. Blade counted fourteen, five of them women. Under the dirt their skins were all various shades of reddish brown, but only a few of them had the green eyes and bluish hair of Kareena and her brother. Some of them were sorting through bulging leather packs, while others squatted by heavy bags slung below long poles.

Bairam wanted to march as he was, but Kareena insisted

21

that he sit down and let her bandage his wounds. Blade noticed that she poured some liquid from a leather bottle onto the bandage, then avoided touching the wound with her bare hands. It was always a relief to find a Dimension where the people had some notion about the causes of infection. Otherwise, if you let the local doctors treat you, you risked dying of blood poisoning. If you tried to treat yourself, you risked being burned for sorcery. Either way was an unpleasant and undignified end.

No one made a move to offer Blade any clothes, so he adjusted his loinguard and sat cross-legged with the spear across his knees until Kareena finished with her brother. Then she pulled out a bone whistle and blew hard. The people with packs strapped them on, those with poles lifted them, and the party moved out. Blade kept toward the front, looking back occasionally for any more signs of the rats. He saw nothing moving, and the hillside soon faded out of sight in the gathering twilight.

Chapter 4

The band of warriors kept going until long after nightfall. They moved surely and swiftly, like people who knew exactly where they were going. After darkness hid the city behind them, they started talking more freely. Blade listened as he marched along.

The warriors were from the city of Kaldak, and Kareena and Bairam were the children of Peython, Kaldak's leader in war and Keeper of the Law. They'd come to Mossev, the city of the towers, to find "Oltec," and found more than they'd expected. Their enemies, the people called the Doimari, didn't claim Mossev, so hadn't taken much from it.

The Kaldakans were satisfied, and were getting ready to make camp among the ruined suburbs when the rats attacked. Apparently the rats had never before attacked in such numbers outside the heart of a city.

Eventually they marched down a steep hillside to the bank of a small stream and made camp. They built an enormous bonfire for warmth and a smaller fire for cooking. Small animals, birds, and even snakes came out of packs, were cut up, then roasted. Someone handed Blade a half-charred bird's wing and a piece of flat hard bread. The bird was gamey and needed salt, and the bread was as hard and tasteless as wood, but Blade was much too hungry to care.

After eating, the Kaldakans tended each other's wounds. Both the men and the women stripped off their clothes to do this, so casually that Blade assumed the Kaldakans had no nudity taboo. Even Kareena stripped, dressed only in boots and her sword belt, and tended her bother's leg. She was much better looking naked than clothed. Her legs were long and powerful, her breasts high, firm, and large-nippled, and all her movements as graceful as a cat's. The triangle of curly hair between her thighs was even bluer than the hair on her head, and the light of the fire brought out the red tinge in her skin. As she moved around the camp, she looked like the bronze statue of a war goddess miraculously brought to life.

Blade felt a tingle of desire as he watched Kareena, but controlled it firmly. Obviously nudity wasn't a sexual invitation in this Dimension. He wondered what was, suspected he'd find out sooner or later, but doubted he'd find out from Kareena. She was the local equivalent of a princess and not the sort of woman to tumble into a man's bed just because he'd saved her baby brother. If she ever came to him, she would come when she wanted to, for her own reasons.

Blade found that he was getting sleepy and decided not to fight it. He had food, warmth, weapons, and a place among people who weren't exactly friends yet but certainly weren't enemies. In some Dimensions he'd started off in prison, as a slave, or wandering in a wilderness filled with dangerous animals. If his travels hadn't taught him anything else, they'd taught him to know when he was well off.

It was a good thing Blade went to sleep early, because Kareena's whistle woke the camp well before dawn. Bairam dug some clothes for Blade out of a pack, and after much trying Blade was able to get into everything except the boots. By the time there was light in the sky, the party was on the move again.

They marched all morning without a pause, with scouts carrying laser rifles well out in front. They'd been confident enough last night to build fires and relax, but now they seemed like a patrol moving through enemy territory. Blade wondered if the enemy they feared was human or animal.

The scouts' rifles didn't go into action that morning. Just before noon they reached a camp of leather tents. There were also more than twenty baggage animals, the munfans, tethered to stakes driven into the ground. The munfans looked like a horse-sized cross between a rabbit and a kangaroo, with long ears and tails and shaggy brown coats with white patches. Their immensely powerful hind legs were armed with long claws, but they seemed docile enough. Each wore a complicated bridle with a long leading rein and a carrying harness dripping with hooks and straps.

The arrival of Kareena's party was the signal for a burst of activity in the camp. Blade was forgotten as the Kaldakans bustled about, striking the tents, tying the packs and bags to the munfans' harnesses, emptying garbage, putting out the campfires, or simply standing guard. Blade noticed that the sentries all carried bows and arrows and spent most of their time looking at the sky. It was another gray day, with a sky full of low-hanging clouds. Blade had no idea what they expected to see coming out of those clouds and everyone was running about too fast to let him ask.

Eventually the bustle died away. Blade saw men kneeling beside each munfan, tying long heavy leather hobbles to brass rings around their hind legs to keep them from taking a full stride. That made sense. Judging from the size of those hind legs, a munfan could run much faster than a man. If an unhobbled munfan bolted, there'd be no way of catching it and no way to save its load other than shooting it.

The last hobbles were being tied into place when Bairam came over to Blade, carrying two laser rifles. He handed one of them to Blade.

"Blade, you saved my life. My honor demands that you carry Oltec, though not living Oltec."

"Your sister—" began Blade, but the boy silenced him with an angry gesture.

"Kareena takes too much on herself. I am not less than she in war or in knowing the Law." Blade seriously doubted this, but it would hardly be tactful to say so.

"This is so," he said quietly. "But my honor as a warrior of England demands that I not break a promise. I have promised Kareena that I will carry no Oltec. Would you have me break my promise to her and lose honor?" He wished he could speak more bluntly. Bairam was rapidly becoming a brave and well-intentioned young nuisance.

"You do not have what Kareena can call a weapon if you carry a dead thing of Oltec that has lost its power," said Bairam insistently. "That is the Law. She can say nothing, yet those who see you will not know that it is dead. This way Kareena's not trusting you will bring you no shame. I cannot have you be shamed. My honor will not let me."

Again Blade wanted to answer bluntly, "Your honor will not let you be quiet either, it seems," but held his tongue. Bairam was going to be stubborn about this, and if Blade argued much longer Kareena or Hota would notice that something was going on. Then there would be another quarrel for everyone. Short of turning Bairam over his knee and spanking him, Blade didn't see there was anything he could do except make the best of a bad situation.

"I thank you, for your care for my honor. I will take this dead Oltec and care for it as though it lived." He took the laser rifle and for lack of any better idea went through the British Army's manual of arms with it. Bairam watched, fascinated.

"Now, I will go to Kareena and explain this," said Blade, when he'd finished. "She must—"

"Oh, no. I will tell her myself. If there is to be another

25

quarrel, I must not let you suffer for it. More honor and many kills, Blade of England." Before Blade could reply, the boy turned and ran off, so fast that Blade couldn't have called to him without letting the whole camp hear. He felt like throwing the rifle to the ground in frustration but knew that would not be a good idea if Oltec really was sacred. At least the damned rifle had a sling, so he could carry it across his chest while he carried the spear on one shoulder.

Whatever Kareena said to her brother, she didn't bother saying anything to Blade. Her whistle shrilled again, the man leading the first munfan jerked the rein, and once more the Kaldakans were on the move. Blade brought up the rear, along with two men carrying rifles and three more carrying bows and arrows. He noticed that the riflemen carried their weapons at the ready, the archers had their bows strung, and all five were watching the sky. Blade watched the munfans instead.

Without the hobbles they certainly would have been out of control within minutes and out of sight soon after that. Their hind claws threw up gravel and clods of earth, while their tails flicked back and forth through long arcs, hard enough to break bone if they hit a man. The carrying harnesses creaked and jingled and the heavy packs and bags bounced so that Blade expected at any minute to see one burst open or fall to the ground.

By mid-afternoon blue sky was showing overhead, but there were still wide patches of gray cloud to hide whatever the Kaldakans feared in the sky. Twice Kareena came back along the caravan but hardly looked at Blade. He began to wish he'd done something to protect his feet. The ground underfoot was getting stony and rough, and even his tough soles were taking punishment.

Another hour or so, and Kareena's whistle signaled a break. The men leading the munfans led them down to a pond to drink, then turned them loose along the bank to graze on ferns and grass. Blade was watching them munch busily, when he heard someone shout. He turned and saw a sentry pointing up into the sky. Following the man's gesture, Blade saw three hawklike birds circling low over the grazing munfans. They flew gracefully, and as they banked

26

Blade saw golden patches under their wings and on their bellies. Handsome birds, but what was all the excitement about?

Then one of the birds flew *into* the clouds, and suddenly Blade realized they weren't flying low at all. He guessed that if they looked so large up near the clouds, their wings must have a spread of twelve feet from tip to tip.

Blade didn't believe that figure at first, then he watched the birds again and decided that fifteen feet would be a better guess. Of course a bird that size was a theoretical impossibility, but he didn't know enough about this Dimension yet to be sure how much Home Dimension theory applied. There could be mutations, there could have been genetic engineering, the birds might be robots. . . .

Meanwhile, none of the Kaldakans seemed to be worrying about theory. They were getting ready to meet the birds. Blade saw the archers picking arrows and the riflemen unslinging their weapons. Meanwhile the people with swords and spears were spreading out into a circle around the munfans, to keep them from bolting. Blade started over to join them, since his only usable weapon was his spear. This was going to be a long-range fight.

Then a rifleman ran up, carrying a second laser under one arm. Blade recognized Sidas, who'd brought him the spear yesterday. "Here, Blade," said the man. "Your Oltec seems to be dead. Since you can carry one now, you should have a live one." He pushed the second laser into Blade's hands and hurried off to rejoin his comrades before Blade could either thank him or protest. After a moment's hesitation Blade followed Sidas toward the other riflemen. He certainly wasn't going to waste time arguing with Kareena or Hota now!

As Blade joined the riflemen, the giant hawks swept low over the caravan with harsh cries. The munfans squealed and some of them danced about as wildly as if the ground under them was red-hot. One tried to break through the circle, but two men drove it back with the butts of their spears.

The birds came over a second time, and now several archers notched arrows and shot. Blade saw two arrows strike home, but the birds flew steadily on until they were out of range. Blade heard Kareena cursing the archers who'd shot, and he hoped his laser had plenty of power. Those birds were going to take a lot of punishment. He also wondered why some of the riflemen hadn't opened up already. Feathers could burn, even if the laser beam didn't get through to a vital organ.

Then the three birds were banking in a wide turn, sliding down until they were just above the treetops, and coming back again. They were enormous, and they were coming straight at Blade. He knelt, raising his rifle. Bowstrings thrummed, arrows whistled, and one of the birds let out a harsh screech. Two more panic-stricken munfans charged the men around them. Blade saw the middle bird growing steadily larger, curled his finger around the trigger—

"Blade, no! You can't!"

Blade recognized the voice shouting. It was Bairam. He ignored him. The bird grew until it filled his whole field of vision. He saw a gaping hooked beak two feet long, red eyes glow into his, the great wings thrashing the air with a rippling hiss. His finger squeezed the trigger, and the world vanished in searing green light as the laser beam leaped out of the rifle straight into the bird's open beak.

The bird never knew what hit it. It flew on for a few feet, then did a somersault in midair and landed belly-upward practically at Blade's feet. Its talons jerked a few times, one wing twitched, then it was dead. Blade stepped forward, wanting to study the wound made by the laser. He was about to sling his rifle and bend over when somebody grabbed him by the shoulder. At the same time he felt a sword point in his back, and heard Hota's angry voice.

"Blade! In the name of the Law, I declare—"

Blade's reflexes took over. He twisted away from the sword point and out from under the clutching hand. At the same time he raised the rifle butt, ready for a stroke. As he whirled to face Hota, he slammed the butt down on the man's sword arm. Hota's fingers opened nervelessly and his sword fell to the ground. He was opening his mouth to shout when Blade drove the rifle butt into his stomach. His mouth stayed open as he writhed on the ground, but no sound came out.

Blade returned his rifle to firing position, then heard

Kareena's voice. "Bairam, you fool! You gave him live Oltec and now he's used it against the Law *twice!*"

"I gave him a *dead* Oltec, Kareena."

"I don't believe you. And if you did, then who—"

"Don't call me a liar, or—"

Another voice, "I saw Sidas give Blade Oltec. He thought—" An incoherent shout, followed by the sounds of a scuffle.

Blade fired the laser into the grass among the munfans. Several of the spearmen ducked, and one of the munfans collapsed out of sheer fright. In the sudden silence Blade was able to speak.

"It seems I've done something wrong. I don't know what it is. I would like someone who does know to tell me, *now!* Meanwhile, everyone else keep quiet, and nobody lays a finger on Sidas. Otherwise I start shooting your munfans."

Kareena gave a wordless snarl and turned to Blade, her eyes wide and mouth working. For a moment he thought she was going to leap on him with her sword. Then she shook all over and began to speak, although her voice trembled with rage.

"Blade, there was no death-danger to you or any of us from that bird. Yet you killed it with Oltec. That is one thing you did against the Law. Then you used Oltec against Hota when he was not using it against you. That is a second thing against the Law.

"For both, the punishment is death. You would die here and now, except for two things. One is that two others aided you in your breaking of the Law. I could punish Sidas here, but not my brother. Also, you are someone my father Peython would like to see before you die. So you will live, as little as you deserve it. Put down your rifle. I have nothing more to say."

Blade saw nods and heard murmurs of agreement. He pointed the muzzle of his rifle at the ground, to make sure no trigger-happy Kaldakan would kill him on the spot. Then he shook his head. "*I* have more to say, Kareena.

"Sidas has done nothing wrong. He gave me living Oltec because he thought I was within the Law. I would have given the Oltec back to him, if he had let me. Sidas has made a mistake, not broken the Law."

He raised the rifle and aimed it at the munfans. Two spearmen almost in the line of fire hastily stepped aside. "I want it sworn here and now that Sidas will not be punished. Otherwise I begin shooting your munfans. I will count to ten, then start shooting. One, two—"

Kareena's lips were bloodless and her voice level. "You will die for that, Blade."

"I am already under a sentence of death, Kareena. Why should it matter to me how soon I die? Also, can you use Oltec to kill me when I am only killing your munfans? I bring no death-danger to *you*." He saw Bairam grin, knew that he'd guessed correctly, and went on briskly. "You can use other weapons to kill me, of course, but not before I kill many of your munfans. Do you want to pay such a price, merely to punish a good man who made a mistake?"

There was a long silence, in which all eyes turned to Kareena. Blade thought some of the Kaldakans were looking at him sympathetically. Then the woman sighed, although her body was still taut and quivering like a bowstring.

"Your honor demands that Sidas go unpunished?"

"It does."

"Then—" She flung her hands wide in disgust. "Very well. If it is your honor at stake . . ." With a heroic effort she steadied herself. "By the Law, I swear that nothing shall be done to Sidas for this day's work. I also swear that your life, limb, and honor shall be safe from me and from all who obey me, until judgment is passed upon you." Her calm broke and she stamped her foot like a small girl having a tantrum. "Is *that* enough for you, Blade of England?"

"It is. In return, I swear to make no attempt to escape, as long as I am under the protection of Kareena, daughter of Peython, leader of the warriors of Kaldak." Holding the laser rifle by the muzzle, he handed it to Kareena.

Blade would have preferred more guarantees of safety but knew he'd won about as much safety as he could hope for. Besides, Hota was back on his feet again and looked ready to attack Blade on the spot, Law or no Law. Blade didn't quite trust Kareena to stop the man if he did. He was alive, they'd accepted his parole, and he suspected that

30

defending Sidas had made him some friends who might guard him from Hota if not from Kareena. For now, this was enough.

Chapter 5

The Kaldakans kept their word about not punishing Sidas and treating Blade honorably. They wouldn't allow him even a knife to cut his food, but didn't bind him. He couldn't fight, but he could run if he had to. He was also fairly sure that if it was really a matter of life or death, many of the fighters would turn a blind eye to his picking up a sword or a bow. He overheard enough remarks praising the way he'd defended Sidas to know that.

No one dared to speak to him openly, for fear of Kareena and Hota. This included Bairam, and this was quite all right with Blade. For now he had nothing polite to say to the boy who'd put his life in danger. He also didn't expect to have anything to say to Hota, who was now clearly Blade's sworn enemy. The man's eyes said everything necessary on that point. Blade would have liked to talk with Kareena and learn more about her father and her city, but could live without this.

Blade settled down to keep up with the Kaldakans as they marched for home. The trip took ten days, and the strips of leather Blade tied around his feet were almost worn through when the city finally came in sight.

Kaldak combined features from Mossev and the ruins he saw when he first arrived in this Dimension. There were three tall towers arranged in a triangle in the center, with nine streets of smaller buildings radiating from the triangle. The buildings on the edge of the city seemed to be storehouses, stables, or workshops. Around the base of the towers were the living quarters and merchants' shops. Damaged buildings had been carefully repaired with timber roofs, leather shutters, stones solidly mortared into place, and lots of paint in vivid colors.

Blade wanted to see more of the city, but Kareena had other ideas. Grim and unsmiling, she marched Blade up the widest street with a drawn sword at his back. Half a dozen fighters followed her, escorting her brother as if he also was a prisoner. Porters with loads, men leading munfans, women carrying laundry, and children playing in the gutters all made way for their chief's daughter. They marched straight up to the base of the nearest of the three towers, then up four flights of broad stairs to the room where Peython, ruler of Kaldak, waited for them.

Peython sat cross-legged on a round wooden table with carved legs, covered with rich gray furs. He wore leather breeches dyed blue, hammered copper bracelets on his wrists and ankles, and an iron-studded belt. Above the waist he wore nothing but a necklace of shiny metal blocks strung on a leather thong. It was almost lost in the hair on his chest. An ugly scar ran diagonally from his left shoulder down across his ribs to his stomach.

Peython's face didn't match the rest of him. It was long, and he had the same expressive green eyes as his children, although his hair was black. His nose was large and hooked, and his mobile lips seemed to smile naturally. He reminded Blade of one of his physics professors at Oxford, suddenly called on to play the part of a barbarian chieftain. Blade wasn't sure he was in the presence of a friend but felt he was in the presence of much wisdom, or at least common sense.

Peython dismissed the guards, then listened in silence while Kareena and Bairam told their stories. Both spoke quickly and clearly, and Bairam seemed much more adult and sensible in his father's presence than he had under his sister's leadership. Perhaps there was a little more to the boy than Blade had suspected.

When Kareena and Bairam were finished, Peython looked at Blade. "Is this true?"

Blade was so surprised at being asked to confirm the

stories of his captors that for a moment he could only nod. Then he added, "I do not think Bairam dares to ask for mercy. I am not sure that Kareena wants her brother to have it." She spun around, but her father's raised hand stopped her before she could speak. "Perhaps you yourself doubt if you should show mercy to your son. If a ruler shows too much mercy to his own children, there are always evil-minded people who cast doubts on his justice or even his wisdom."

"I see you know something of ruling, Blade of England. Were you a chief in England?"

"No, but I was a warrior in the house of a mighty chief who taught me much." That would do for a description of J and MI6A, as well as Lord Leighton and Project Dimension X.

"You are worthy of his teaching. Do you wish me to show mercy to my son in the matter of his going against the Law?"

Blade answered the blunt question simply. "Yes, I do."

"Why do you believe you have any right to speak of this matter?" snapped Kareena. "That is what I want to know. And I want to know why my father—"

"Kareena," said Peython. He did not raise his voice, but again Kareena stopped with her mouth half open. Then she swallowed the rage visible on her face and stood silently.

"That is a good question, when I think upon it," said Peython after a short silence. "Blade, you will answer it."

"I do not *know* that I have any such right," said Blade. "I am a stranger who does not know your Law and may yet die for breaking it. I do know honor, and what it is to a warrior. Your son broke the Law trying to save my honor, by giving me Oltec. I think he was also trying to save the honor of Kaldak. Not giving Oltec to a man who saved the life of its chief's son might be dishonor to the city. Am I right, Bairam?"

The boy could only gape like a dying fish for a moment, then said, "Yes, Father. That is how I thought. Blade has said it better than I could have, though. I thank him for his strong words." Now he looked more like a grateful puppy than a dying fish.

Kareena didn't look grateful. She looked as if she

33

wanted to skin Blade alive with a very dull knife, then roll him in coarse salt. In her father's presence, she would keep a rein on her tongue, but Blade had the unpleasant feeling he'd made another enemy. Having a beautiful woman hating him did not bother him as much as it usually did. It didn't seem as if Kareena would do anything to help him whether she hated him or not!

Peython sat with his chin in one hand for a minute, then stood up and jumped down off the table with the agility of a young man. "I think Blade does speak strong words, also wise ones. But we *are* Kaldak of the Law. We are not Doimar, where the Law is only studied in the hope of finding ways to break it. To let Bairam go unpunished, to let Blade live—this is far beyond the Law. I cannot go so far myself if I want to, nor do I want to.

"Therefore the Gathering shall be proclaimed." Kareena gasped. "In seven times seven days, all of Kaldak shall Gather to hear what I have heard today. When they have heard, they shall give their judgment, and that judgment shall guide me. Do you accept this, Bairam?"

"Yes, and with gratitude, Father."

"Save your gratitude for Blade, if you think it will help him," growled the chief. "Blade, what do you say?"

Apparently Peython was going to leave matters to an assembly of the people of Kaldak, which couldn't be convened for nearly two months. That was a free gift of two months' extra life, and Blade was a great believer in the old saying, "While there's life there's hope." Even a slave can hope to find himself free, while a dead man can do absolutely nothing to improve his situation.

"I accept. I trust the wisdom of the people of Kaldak. I know that if I die, it will not be from their hatred of me, but only because they care for their Law. That is an honorable death, by the Laws of England." He had no intention of passively submitting to that death, however honorable it might be, but there was no need to tell Peython that.

"Very good. Kareena, Bairam, you may go." When his children were gone, Peython sat down again and frowned at Blade. "Blade, why did you speak as you did for Bairam? Kareena is not pleased, and I am curious."

Blade had the feeling that he might throw away most of

Peython's goodwill whatever he said, so he decided to tell the truth. "I do not care whether Kareena likes me or not. If there is such bad feeling between them that she wishes her brother punished, I do not *want* her friendship. It could turn to hatred any day."

"That is true. But that also does not answer my question. Many people would say that Bairam is a fool, and that you are a fool for thinking he is worth anything or can do anything for you."

Blade smiled. "Bairam is no fool, or at least no more of a fool than I was at his age. He is not stupid. If his mistakes do not kill him soon, he will learn. In time, he may even learn enough to be a worthy son to you, and a proper chief for Kaldak, city of the Law.

"He is also honorable, and will be a friend to those who have done him good. I have come to Kaldak, without friends or knowledge of its ways. I need every friend I can honorably win. Do you feel that *I* have lacked honor—?"

He broke off as he saw Peython's frown deepen and his shoulders begin to shake. For a moment he thought he'd finally said too much, then realized that Peython was trying to hide laughter. Finally he sighed and looked at Blade again.

"Blade, men who have known my son since he came from his mother's body have not found such wise words for him. I am going to find your time in Kaldak interesting, however long it lasts and however it ends." He rose and shouted for the guards. "You may go now."

Chapter 6

Blade spent his first few days in Kaldak as something less than a guest but somewhat more than a prisoner. He was confined to a room on the ground floor of the northern tower. The room had heavy wooden bars on the door and a guard armed with a laser rifle at the door, but plenty of light, air, and comfortable furniture. The Kaldakans also fed Blade three large meals a day, along with good strong beer. Once they even brought him a bronze jug of distilled liquor which tasted like cheap gin.

Blade didn't like being confined even as comfortably as this. He was bored, and he wasn't learning anything about Kaldak or getting enough exercise. He also knew that he was still at the Kaldakans' mercy. He did have to admit that if he was going to be a prisoner at all, this was one of the most comfortable prisons he'd ever seen in any Dimension.

On the sixth day Kareena came to him with an escort of guards led by Hota and a message from Peython. "If you give your word of honor not to leave Kaldak, you may go where you will within the city until the Gathering," she said. Her words came out in short bursts from a tight mouth. Obviously she didn't like having to deliver this message.

"I swear by the Law of England and my own honor as a warrior that I shall not put one foot beyond the streets of Kaldak until the Gathering has rendered its judgment," said Blade. He hoped he wouldn't also be asked to swear to submit tamely to a sentence of death. He would rather not have to take an oath he had no intention of keeping. He

36

could lie with a straight face if he had to—his years in MI6A guaranteed that. But he still preferred to tell the truth, particularly among people who took oaths much more seriously than the "civilized" nations of Home Dimension.

"Do we know that England has a Law by which anyone can swear?" asked Hota.

Kareena looked at him sharply, half angry and half embarrassed. "We do not. But we can hardly ask Blade to swear by the Law of Kaldak when he is confined for breaking it."

"Then why take an oath from him at all?"

"Because my father has ordered that we take it," snapped Kareena. "And I will say nothing more on this to you, Hota." She turned and stamped out. Hota lingered a moment to glower at Blade, then followed her. Blade frowned and poured himself some beer. At least Peython's order hadn't made him any new enemies. But he'd have to watch his back carefully as he moved around Kaldak. Hota would cheerfully slit his throat for a penny, and might be a formidable opponent even in a straight fight.

It turned out that Blade didn't have to worry about his back. Bairam appointed himself Blade's official escort from the first day of Blade's parole. With the chief's son and heir by his side, Blade could go anywhere he wanted in the city without anyone trying to stop him. Accidents were another matter. Bairam was as impulsive as ever, and sometimes Blade wondered who was keeping whom out of trouble.

In spite of this, Blade quickly learned most of what he wanted to know about Kaldak. Peython ruled about twelve thousand people. Most of them lived in the buildings of the city itself, including the farmers who went out to their fields every morning and returned every night. The rest were herdsmen who lived in distant pastures with their herds and flocks, or fishermen who lived by the Aloga River. The herds and fish gave Kaldak plenty of meat, and the rich soil of its fields produced grain and vegetables. The people of Kaldak were mostly slim-bodied, but it was not for lack of food.

37

"It is said that our land is richer than that of many cities because we keep the Law better than they do," said Bairam.

"Do you believe this?" asked Blade.

"Is it possible that it is—not so?"

"Many things are possible, for I have seen them since I left England," said Blade. "But I have not seen enough of Kaldak to answer that question." He didn't want to get into a full-scale discussion. For one thing, Kaldak probably had some punishment for questioning the Law's principles. For another thing, the less he said himself, the more freely Bairam would talk.

"I think the Law makes some difference," said Bairam. "We eat better and we have found more living Oltec. But our women bear no more children than those of cities with a weaker Law."

That answered one of Blade's questions—why there were so few children. Some lingering aftereffect of the war—radiation, chemicals, a plague—made men or women or both infertile. When you had to do most work by muscle-power, a small and slowly-growing population was a very mixed blessing. When you had to do most of your fighting with muscle-powered weapons, it was an outright curse.

The Kaldakans despised those cities with a weak Law and the wretched Tribes with no Law at all, who lived by hunting and gathering in the forests. But they could not ignore them. The warriors of Kaldak were always meeting the warriors of Doimar and its allies in savage fights over new finds of Oltec in the ruined cities. Over the years these fights took their toll of Kaldak's best men. Even more warriors died in fights with the Tribes when they raided Kaldak's fields or herds or burned the fishermen's huts.

Other cities had strong Laws and were more or less friendly. Kaldak traded with some of them, and there was a whole street of merchants supported by this trade. They sold leather, metal, furs, bone implements, drinking cups, weapons, fire jewels—

"Fire jewels?" asked Blade. He hadn't heard the term before.

"You've seen my father's necklace, haven't you?" said Bairam. "That is made of fire jewels."

Blade remembered Peython's necklace of small metal blocks strung on a leather thong. "Why are they called fire jewels?"

"Because they hold fire within them, they cannot be cut or worked like other kinds of jewels or metal things of the Oltec. If you cut into them, they burst with much bright blue light or melt with a sound like meat frying. If a man holds them too long, he feels as though he is being struck by lightning. Men have died from holding burning fire jewels. Do you know why this is so?"

"I do not," said Blade, which was only partly the truth. "But I would very much like to look closely at some fire jewels." That was a considerable understatement.

"Well, there is a merchant of fire jewels named Saorm, and indeed I was going to visit his house tomorrow," said Bairam. He hesitated. "I was not going to ask you to come with me—you see, I have a rather special reason for going there—"

"Is it his wife or his daughter?"

"You are very clever, Blade. Yes, it is his daughter Geyrna."

"And—you do not think her father approves?"

"I do not know. I think he would not keep away the chief's son, but Geyrna is only fifteen." He shrugged. "We keep swearing to ourselves that next time we will tell him, but somehow we always forget." He smiled. "Geyrna is very pretty. She has red hair, which is not common in the Land."

"I see." By now Blade understood enough about Kaldak to understand the sexual customs here. The Kaldakans didn't worry about nudity because they didn't worry about sexual fidelity. Any man could ask any woman for sex, and an adult woman could ask any man. A married woman needed only her husband's consent to have sex with another man, and an unmarried girl under seventeen needed only her father's permission. This leniency regarding sexual activity was the only way the Kaldakans had to make sure that all the fertile men and fertile women sooner or later got together and produced enough children to keep up the population of the city. If a woman bore a child to someone not her husband, it was still her husband's heir, but the actual father could also claim the honor of "Protector." That way all of Kaldak's precious children had at least one father, and many of them had two.

Having sex with a young girl without her father's permission was not precisely a violation of the Law itself, but it was definitely frowned on. Saorm probably would not object to the chief's son becoming the father of his grandchild, but other people would certainly talk. Blade was quite sure Peython was quite tired of his son's doing things to make people talk. He was also sure that the chief would be happy if he kept Bairam out of Geyrna's bed, for he had not yet met her nor had a chance to approve of her.

If Blade tried to keep the young man away from Geyrna, however, Bairam wouldn't take him to the fire jewels. He suspected they were far more important to the future of Kaldak and the whole Dimension than one girl's virtue or what people would say. He also suspected that to obtain the fire jewels he would have to break the Law again. Blade recalled the old saying, "They can only hang you once," and refused to worry.

"I'll come with you to Saorm's house," said Blade. "After that I'll turn my back, if you'll do the same."

"Thank you, Blade. I swear to do as you wish."

They went to Saorm's house late in the morning, in the hope of finding the man out doing his shopping. He was a widower, and his daughter kept house for him.

They were lucky. The house was empty except for Geyrna and the slave who did the heavy work. The girl looked much older than fifteen, and she was not only beautiful but clearly delighted to see Bairam. In fact, she looked ready to tear his clothes off right in front of Blade. Bairam led her off to the back of the shop, the slave went out to draw water from the well, and Blade was left alone with the fire jewels.

They were all rectangular blocks of metal, three times as long as they were wide, with a small ring on one end. They came in a number of sizes, the smallest about three inches long and the largest nearly a foot. Blade studied them carefully. They might be what he suspected, but he'd need a piece of Oltec to prove it. He started looking.

Fortunately most prosperous houses in Kaldak had a piece of dead Oltec somewhere, as a kind of household totem. In a few minutes Blade found the merchant's piece, a pistol-shaped object with a hollow metal tube sticking out of the muzzle. Blade couldn't tell if it was a weapon or a tool but knew there should be a place for the "fire jewels" somewhere in it, if he was right. There was definitely a switch on the top.

He started poking and prying at the "pistol." At last he felt something give. With his thumbnail he pried open a corroded metal cover on the handle, exposing a rectangular slot the exact size and shape of the smallest fire jewels. Blade snatched one off the table, held his breath, and tried to insert it into the slot.

It slipped easily into place.

Now Blade pointed the muzzle at the ceiling, then thumbed the switch forward. For a moment many years of dirt and corrosion resisted. Then the switch snapped forward.

With a shrill whine, the metal tube started to turn.

Blade let out a war-whoop of triumph and danced around the room, waving the tool until he collided with the table, which promptly fell over with a crash. Blade ignored the pain in his shins. He'd never had the sensation of holding in his hands the whole future of a Dimension before. He felt almost drunk with delight.

As he'd suspected, the fire jewels were miniature power storage cells, far beyond anything in Home Dimension technology. Inserted into "dead" Oltec, they could make it "live" again. The Kaldakans and the other cities of the Land would have more tools and weapons than they'd ever dreamed of. Then if they could find a way to recharge the power cells . . .

Yes, but how many of the fire jewels were there, and how many still held power? Blade realized that he didn't know, and the realization sobered him. So did the appearance of Bairam and Geyrna, drawn by the uproar he'd made. Both were stark naked, but they looked so contented that Blade knew he hadn't interrupted their lovemaking too

41

soon. The girl smiled and shook her head so that her long dark red hair fell down over her bare shoulders. Then she saw what Blade was holding, and her smiled faded.

"England-man Blade, that is—" Blade flipped the switch and the tool's whine filled the room. "That is—it was *dead*. Bairam! It was dead! Now it *lives*! But—" She didn't have the words for what she wanted to say. Bairam put an arm around her and comforted her, although his own face was twisting and his mouth hanging open.

"Bairam!" said Blade sharply. "Where is there a dead Oltec weapon I can have?"

"You can't have—the Law—" Bairam now seemed to be nearly as confused as Geyrna.

"I must see if I can make other dead Oltec live," said Blade as patiently as he could. "It is most important to make the weapons live again—"

"Yes," said Bairam, understanding dawning on his face. "If you make Oltec live again, then the Law must be changed. What you did to the greathawk will be no breaking of the Law, not if there is more than enough live Oltec to go around. And you—"

"Will not have a death sentence hanging over my head," finished Blade, grinning at the boy. Whatever faults Bairam might have, he certainly wasn't stupid. "Now— *where is an Oltec weapon?*"

"In my rooms in my father's house," said the boy. "I have two of them. One is not only dead but hurt. The other maybe you could make—live again." He said the words as if he still couldn't quite believe them, then turned to the girl. "Geyrna, I must—"

At this moment Saorm the merchant walked in. He took one step into his shop, then stopped. Bairam bolted out the door, not bothering to put on his clothes. Geyrna knelt, murmuring "Oh, the Law protect us, the Law protect us." Blade lifted the tool and turned it on. As he saw his household totem of dead Oltec coming to life, the man's eyes bulged until Blade thought they would fall out of his head. Blade scooped up a handful of the fire jewels, turned off the tool, and put it down by the fallen table. Then he followed Bairam out the door before Saorm could recover from his confusion.

42

Chapter 7

Although Bairam was running fast, Blade caught up with him before they were out of sight of Saorm's door. He seized the boy by the arm and whispered fiercely, "Slow down, you young idiot! If you run, everyone will notice you. We don't want that until we've tested the rifles."

"Yes, but if we don't hurry, Geyrna's father will spread the word all over Kaldak. I think what you've done breaks the Law and—"

"If you hadn't bolted like a frightened munfan, we wouldn't have to worry about Saorm! We could have stayed and told him what we'd done. Then he might have kept his mouth shut. As it is—" Blade made a gesture of utter disgust.

The boy sighed. "I am sorry, Blade. But—I could not think as I should have. I—"

"I know. Well, not much harm was done this time. But you're going to have to think first and *then* act, from now on. Do I have your word of honor on that?"

"Yes, Blade."

They returned to Peython's tower without attracting any attention or hearing any unusual uproar behind them. Blade hoped that Saorm was on his knees along with his daughter, and would stay there for a while.

The two rifles in Bairam's rooms each had a slot in the butt, about the right size for one of the six-inch fire jewels. The slot of one rifle was a cracked and corroded mess. Blade scraped the other slot clean with a knife and dropped the fire jewel into place. Then he raised the rifle, mentally crossed his fingers, and pulled the trigger.

43

Fzzzzzzztttt!

A beam of dazzling green light as thick as Blade's thumb lanced across the room. On the far wall a six-inch circle turned black. Smoke curled up and hot bits of stone sprayed the room. Blade fired again, the smoke made him cough, and now there was a hole in the wall several inches deep.

Blade turned to Bairam, who was trying not to look excited and almost succeeding. "The fire jewels in the Oltec must have lost power faster than the ones used as ornaments—" he began. Then he realized that Bairam was staring at him without understanding. Oh, well, time enough to explain electricity later. Right now they needed more experiments.

"We must have more of the fire jewels," said Blade. "Do you know if there are any more in—"

"There's my father's necklace," said Bairam eagerly. "I'm sure he wouldn't mind—"

"I'm sure he *would* mind," said Blade, heading off the boy's enthusiasm. "Any others?"

Bairam shook his head, then said reluctantly. "You don't want me to go back to Saorm, do you?"

Blade nodded. "We need those fire jewels, Bairam. And you are a warrior of Kaldak."

Blade's hint was enough. The boy pulled on some clothes and hurried out the door. A minute later he came back, much faster than he'd left. Right after him came Kareena.

She was wearing only knee-length trousers and a sword, and Blade thought her bare breasts were even lovelier than before. He also thought she was angrier than he'd ever seen her. Her face was an icy mask except for the eyes, which blazed like hot coals, and her voice shook.

"Blade, you are going to *die*. Brother, you deserve to, even though you probably won't. Our father is weak enough to think—"

"You will *not* speak of our father that way, Kareena," snapped Bairam. He started to draw his sword, then remembered he wasn't wearing one. Blade cautiously shifted his position to where he could cover the open door with the rifle, without any danger of hitting Kareena or her brother.

"I will speak as I please, and you will not stop me. Not

44

after throwing the Law into the pigsties with this Blade, giving him live Oltec a *second* time—"

"I did not give him live Oltec. He—"

"I will not believe you. You—"

"Kareena, only blood will wipe out what you just said. Let me get a sword and—"

"SHUT UP, BOTH OF YOU!"

Blade's roar silenced them as completely as if he'd shot them both dead. "Thank you," he said. "Now, you are going to listen. Bairam, stop threatening your sister. She has only made a mistake. When she learns that, she will apologize. In the meantime I want no more talk of shedding her blood. I will break your arms before I let you touch her. Do you understand?"

"Yes, Blade," said Bairam, unnaturally subdued.

"Good. Kareena, what I have done today may be so important that the meaning of the Law perhaps has to be changed. I have found a way to make dead Oltec live again."

"You have—*no!* That is impossible."

"It is not impossible, Kareena," said Bairam quietly. "I have seen it myself. Look at the Oltec he holds. That is the dead piece which hung on my wall, isn't it?"

Kareena stepped closer and looked at the rifle in Blade's hands. "Yes. I—I recognize the marks."

"And you knew it was dead?"

"Yes. By the Law, it was dead."

"But Blade had made it live again. Take it from Blade, Kareena, and use it. You will see."

Blade had doubts about the wisdom of letting someone in Kareena's mood have a live weapon, but he let her take the rifle. She raised it, aimed it out into the hall, and fired.

Fzzzztttt!

Another bolt of green fire, this one just missing two servants passing with armloads of pots. They screamed, dropped their loads, and ran off down the hall.

Kareena stood with the rifle in her hands, shaking all over, eyes squeezed shut. Blade saw tears trickling out from under her eyelids, gently took the rifle from her, and handed it to Bairam. Then he took her in his arms and held her as he would have held a hurt child, although he

45

was very conscious of the fine breasts pressing against his chest.

Kareena fought not to cry in front of Blade and her brother. Finally she stepped away from Blade and wiped her eyes with the back of one hand. Then she smiled. "I am sorry, Blade. For my anger and for my weakness. I do not know what you have done—it reaches deep into me. Now I wonder if indeed you are sent to Kaldak by the Sky Masters."

The smile lit up her whole face. It could not make her thin features truly beautiful, but it made them enormously *alive*. For Blade that was more important than picture-book beauty. He smiled back. "Kareena, I did what I did because I have a busy mind and prying fingers. If I had not opened a new future for Kaldak when I started prying into the Oltec, you might have had reason to attack me."

"Perhaps. But . . ." Her smile faded.

"Don't torture yourself over what's past," said Blade briskly. "And keep smiling. You look much better smiling than when you look as though you would geld me on the spot if you had a knife!"

Bairam laughed. "Kareena, will you now believe me when I say that? Blade, I've told her many times that she could have six husbnds if she only smiled a little. But no—she will look like the spirit of plague!"

Kareena sighed. "Bairam, if you talked less I might believe you more. I know that you tell the truth half the time. But *which* half?"

Blade hated to break up this reconciliation between Kareena and her brother, but he knew time was short. "Kareena, Bairam, I think it would be wise if we got some beer, then sat down while you told me all about how the Land came to be the way it is. We must put everything that has happened today before your father Peython. Otherwise Saorm will spread tales all over Kaldak. Even if there is no panic, the tales may reach ears which should not hear them.

"Right now I do not know enough about this city and the Land to be sure I will not appear foolish before your father. I do not want to appear foolish before him. He is not the man to forgive that, I think."

The other two agreed heartily. Servants brought the beer, Kareena poured out three cups, and Blade settled down to listen to the history of this Dimension. There were few surprises, but a lot of things he'd already known made more sense after listening to Bairam and Kareena.

This Dimension once had an advanced civilization. Its people were sometimes called the Sky Masters, because they had flown through the sky in great machines, and sometimes the Tower Builders, because of the towers in their cities.

Whatever they were called, they destroyed their civilization in a great war. Atomic and hydrogen bombs, lasers, radioactive dust, bacteria, chemicals, and exotic war machines were all used. Many cities were destroyed, and most of the rest made uninhabitable.

Only the people in the mountains and on the most remote farms survived the war. It left many of them sterile, and too many of the babies born were horrible mutations. After a few generations of ruthlessly killing the worst mutations, the human stock was almost back to normal. Those mutations which remained, such as the blue hair of Kareena and Bairam, were considered marks of honor. Other animals were less fortunate. Some of the animal mutations were useful, such as the munfans. Other were a menace, including the greathawks and the giant rats.

After several more generations, the radioactivity and chemicals faded away. People came from the mountains and the farms and tried to rebuild civilization in those cities which still stood. They found much of the Sky Masters' machinery still intact, but the knowledge of how to build or repair it was gone. When a piece of the Old Technology— shortened to Old Tech, then corrupted to Oltec—wore out, it could not be fixed. Some brave men and women tried to repair dead Oltec, but many of them died in accidents and learned nothing.

Slowly the supply of Oltec shrank, as one piece of equipment after another died. Slowly the cities began to fight over what was left. Slowly the Law emerged in most cities, slightly different in each one but with two points in common almost everywhere.

First, Oltec could be used only in the most desperate

situations, when life or something equally valuable was in danger. Second, no one should try to repair a piece of Oltec or use any Oltec machine which wasn't lying around ready for the taking. The people of the Land would seldom climb the towers to look for it, and never went into cellars. Oltec not lying around ready at hand was Oltec they were not meant to use.

Everyone knew that in time there would be no more Oltec to take from the ruins of the cities. Everyone was afraid of what might happen then. Everyone knew that trying to go outside the Law would make matters worse. Under the Law, Blade was actually guilty of two capital offenses: using Oltec unnecessarily and trying to repair it.

"If you hadn't discovered the secret of the fire jewels, I do not think even our father could have kept you alive until the Gathering," said Kareena grimly. "The people would storm this tower and tear you to pieces in front of his eyes, and set a new chief in his place if he tried to speak against it."

"They may still try it, if Saorm tells the city before we talk to our father," said Bairam. "Blade, have you heard enough so that you can stand before him?"

"I have."

"Good. Then let us go to him." He rose, and Blade noted that the boy was gone, at least for the moment. In his place was a sober, quiet young man. Blade wondered if it was the rivalry with Kareena which had brought out the worst in Bairam. He certainly hoped this new maturity would last.

Chapter 8

Peython quickly understood the importance of Blade's discovery. Before Blade could even finish his story, Peython summoned his guards.

"Go to the house of Saorm the merchant in fire jewels," he told them. "Bring him and his daughter Geyrna here at once. Do not harm them, but do not let them resist you or delay you. If anyone questions you on the way, say that Saorm is suspected of giving aid to Doimar."

After the guards left, Peython glowered at his son. "If the Doimari learn about this because you lost your head, *you* will be guilty of aiding them. I'm not going to punish you for that, but I will hardly forget it either. Now continue your story, Blade."

Blade did so. Peython let him finish, then asked Kareena and Bairam to tell their versions. When all three were finished, Peython squatted cross-legged on his table and seemed to be meditating. Neither his children nor Blade dared to interrupt him. Before he'd finished his meditations, the guards returned with Saorm and Geyrna. Peython dismissed the guards again and listened to Saorm tell his story.

Much to everyone's relief, the merchant had told no one of what he'd seen. He'd been too busy praying to the Sky Masters, the Spirit of the Law, the Lord of the Towers, and anyone else he thought might listen. He was barely able to believe what he'd seen and was quite sure he'd never be able to make anyone else believe it. Since she was already in her father's bad graces for her affair with Bairam, Geyrna hadn't dared move a step or say a word without his permission.

When the man was finished, Peython said, "You have done nothing against the Law. You will do nothing against my pleasure, as long as you are silent about what you saw today."

"I can do this, Peython. But what about my daughter and your son?"

Peython smiled as he studied the girl. "I have decided that you must give your permission for your daughter to see Bairam. I will have Bairam follow the Law if Geyrna bears his child, of course. Otherwise I think it best we save our words until they are needed."

Both Bairam and Geyrna looked happy at Peython's words. The merchant shrugged, apparently realizing that he had no say in the matter and that the interview had come to an end. "Come, Geyrna." He was reaching for her hand when she suddenly jumped back.

"Tell them about the fire jewels of Gilmarg! Tell them where they are and why you hid them, Father!"

"What are you talking about?" the man snarled, but Blade saw his eyes flicker and his tongue come out. Blade moved close to him and signaled Kareena to do the same.

"You hid enough fire jewels to bring life to all the Oltec in Kaldak, because you and your friends wanted a good price for—"

"Peython, my daughter is lying! You can't believe—"

Peython stood up. Suddenly he no longer looked quite so much like a professor playing the part of a barbarian chieftain. His face showed the same cold rage Blade was used to seeing on Kareena's. Bairam drew his sword and stood close to Geyrna. Saorm looked at all the grim faces around him and swallowed hard.

"My son, who knows your daughter well, does not think she is lying," said Peython. "My daughter, who is wise beyond her years, does not think she is lying. Blade of England, who has seen many lands, does not think she is lying. I myself, chief of Kaldak, do not think she is lying." He jumped down from the table and walked up to the merchant.

50

His voice softened. "You have done no harm *yet*. When you found these jewels, you could not have known their secret. They were no more than pretty things you bought and sold. Now they are more. They are the future of Kaldak and perhaps of all the Land. *They are no longer yours.* So where are they?"

The merchant's mouth hardened, although sweat was breaking out on his forehead. "And if I do not choose to tell?"

At a signal from her father, Kareena put the bar in place across the door. "Among us, I think we know enough to make any man talk," said Peython. "After that—well, wagging tongues can be cut out. Hands which reach for what belongs to other men can be cut off. Eyes which see only greed can be put out."

The merchant started trembling so hard Blade was afraid he might faint on the spot. "Come, Saorm," said Blade more gently. "The only way you can keep your secret now is by killing yourself. We might not let you do that. Even if you succeeded, you would get no profit from your discovery. If you tell us what we want to know, I at least think you should have some reward."

"M-m-my life?" said Saorm.

"Yes," said Peython. "Perhaps more. But *start talking!*"

Now that he'd found himself with no choice but to talk, Saorm could hardly get the words out fast enough. When he'd finished, Kareena asked, "Does anyone else know where these jewels are?"

"No, lady. Only me. The stone I pushed into the mouth of the tunnel—one man could move it. I swear it, by the Sky Masters!"

"We believe you, Saorm," said Peython. "If you hold your tongue and guide my men to the jewels, I will even reward you. For now, you will be my guest. I will also take your daughter and your slave into my care." He sounded the gong for his guards.

After they'd taken Saorm out, the chief turned to the others. "We have won ourselves some time, but not much. The sooner we send men to Gilmarg, the better. But I think we shall speak more wisely after some food. Geyrna, will you accept a place at my table?"

51

The girl flushed and looked at the floor. "I would be honored, Peython."

The dinner was supposed to be a planning session for the expedition to Gilmarg, to bring home Saorm's roomful of fire jewels. Instead it became a celebration of Blade's discovery, the bright new future it opened for Kaldak, and all the other discoveries he might make in the future. The table creaked under the weight of platters of meat, and the beer and liquor went around and around, one toast after another.

The liquor still tasted like gin to Blade. Now it seemed like good Bombay gin, not the sort of cheap rotgut sold in dockside pubs. Kareena slid lower and lower in her chair and sometimes broke into song. It was always a relief when she stopped. She had a lovely speaking voice but couldn't carry a tune in a bucket. Geyrna giggled a lot and leaned openly on Bairam's shoulder, while he held her up and caressed her. Only Peython seemed to remain completely sober, although he drank half again as much as anyone else in the room. For all the effect the liquor had on him, he might have been drinking fruit juice.

At last Bairam and Geyrna staggered off to his room, both nearly naked and their arms around each other's waist. Kareena was having trouble standing up, so Blade went over to help her. She sprang up like a jack-in-the-box, then leaned against him and raised her face to him. The invitation in her eyes was unmistakable. Blade bent and kissed her. For a moment her lips flared wide and hot, her seeking tongue darting out to meet his. Then she jerked as if she'd gripped one of the power cells, and she twisted away from Blade. He watched her lurch off to her room, and he was very conscious of Peython watching him.

Blade reached his own room, to find the door unlocked and the guard gone. He was beginning to drift off to sleep when he heard a knock on the door. Before he could move, the door opened and he saw Geyrna silhouetted against the light in the hall. She carried a fur robe over one arm, but otherwise she was stark naked. Her red hair tumbled down wildly, almost reaching her buttocks.

"Geyrna, what are you doing here?"

52

She giggled. "I have come to make you Bairam's brother. What else did you think, Blade of England?" She patted one full breast and the patch of red hair between her legs.

"Ah," said Blade. If two men who'd fought side by side in battle also had sex with the same woman, this gave them a form of brotherhood under the Law. Blade wasn't entirely sure he wanted to be any sort of kin to the hotheaded Bairam, but he could hardly insult both the chief's son and the girl by flatly refusing. Before he could even think of any words to delay matters, Geyrna darted across the room, swept the blankets off the bed, and leaped on top of Blade.

"Ah," he said again, this time in a very different tone of voice. The girl seemed to be kissing or caressing every part of his body at once. Her warm smooth skin and the musk of her own arousal made Blade aggressively ready for her almost at once. She was starting to kiss his throbbing penis when he gripped her shoulders and rolled her off him. Then he bent over her, kissing her lips, letting his tongue and hers dance together while he stroked her breasts. Nipples like miniature spear points tickled his palms, and he heard Geyrna moan. He trailed fingers across her pubic hair, felt dampness, heard her moan louder. Then he raised himself above her and entered.

Her thighs and legs clamped around him as if he was her only hold on the world. Her nails dug into the skin of his shoulders, and he heard her sobbing breath in his ear. He thrust steadily, with increasing eagerness as his own self-control began to go. He wanted to hold back, but he also wanted to ease the exquisite agony slowly turning every part of his body to fire.

Blade's breath tore its way out of his throat in a long gasp at the same moment as Geyrna cried out. Blade knew that half the tower could have heard her and didn't care. He sagged forward, the strength oozing out of his arms. It was all he could do to keep from settling down on her with his whole two hundred and ten pounds of now thoroughly limp muscle and bone.

She lay beside him, one nipple brushing his elbow and one hand resting on his groin. "Now you and Bairam are brothers," she said quietly. "You will be even more his brother if you bed Kareena. I think she will have you if you ask her."

Blade doubted this but was too tired to find words easily. By the time he'd thought of an answer Geyrna's even breathing told him that she was sound asleep. Blade pulled the blankets over both of them and closed his eyes.

Blade didn't wake up until well after dawn. By then Geyrna was gone, and his head was throbbing with a ferocious hangover. By the time he'd washed and shaved, he felt ready to face Peython and the others.

Either Peython had stayed awake all night or got up very early. Even more annoying, he still showed no signs of all his drinking. That was more than could be said of his son, Geyrna, or Kareena, who wobbled in last of all, obviously nursing a hangover even worse than Blade's.

They quickly unrolled a map of the Land and made their plans. Saorm would lead them to where the fire jewels were hidden, and Kareena, Bairam, and Blade would take fifty fighting men and women and twenty munfans to Gilmarg. That was all Kaldak could spare at the moment, although there might be enough fire jewels and other valuable Oltec to load every munfan the city had.

"Gilmarg is also in land claimed by Doimar," said Peython. "The last time we sent men to Gilmarg, the Doimari killed many of them. The same thing could happen again. I would not be sending either of you or Blade if I had a choice, but—"

"You have no choice," said Bairam, with unexpected dignity. "And we have the duty of proving ourselves worthy children of Peython of Kaldak."

Bairam and Kareena would in theory be leaders of the expedition, with Blade serving them. In fact, Blade would be a third leader.

"And you will both swear to listen to his advice," said Peython sharply.

"Yes, Father," his children chorused.

Blade would teach them all he knew about Oltec, then let them do all the actual work with it. "Under the Law, Blade, you cannot touch Oltec—or carry any weapon—

until the Gathering gives its judgment. Even I could not set the Law aside without making many tongues wag. Then we might lose all we have gained."

The "cover story" for the expedition was mostly the truth. In Gilmarg there was a great hoard of fire jewels. If enough could be brought home to Kaldak, Peython would ask the Gathering to allow wise men to study the fire jewels. This would prepare everyone for a possible change in the Law, without giving away the secret of Blade's discovery.

Kareena looked at the map and traced the march from Kaldak to Gilmarg with her forefinger. "This should be easy enough. It is a short journey."

"It is the longest journey ever made by men of Kaldak, daughter," said Peython. "It is a journey from the past of the Land into its future."

Chapter 9

From the top of the tree where Blade was perched, the city of Gilmarg looked like a smaller, more battered edition of Mossev. Two of its eighteen towers were only piles of rubble, and the rest had lost most of their color and ornament. Tall trees grew up through the paving of some streets, and vines choked many of the doors and lower-floor windows. There was no sign of human life. Although the Doimari claimed Gilmarg, it was far enough from Doimar so they didn't keep a permanent garrison in it.

Blade sat up, straddled the branch, and shouted down to the people on the ground eighty feet below. "No sign of the Doimari!"

A voice floated up through the needles. "Would Blade

recognize a Doimari if he saw one? Best that I go forward and see."

That could only be Hota. He couldn't be denied a place on the expedition. He was a leading warrior of Kaldak, who'd been to Gilmarg several times before. This honor hadn't improved his manners. He considered being obliged to associate with Blade an insult, and being obliged to take Bairam's and Kareena's orders was almost as bad. He said whatever he pleased whenever he pleased and seemed to be hoping to provoke Blade or Bairam into a quarrel. Sooner or later, he was going to succeed with Bairam.

Blade scrambled down the tree too late to hear what anyone said to Hota. Hota and four other fighters were already on their way toward the edge of the forest and Gilmarg. Blade was relieved to hear that one of them was Sidas. He at least would keep his eyes open enough to keep Hota from returning and talking nonsense. For a while there was nothing for Blade to do except join the men who were cutting ferns for the munfans. As a man outside the Law, he wasn't allowed to carry a weapon, so he couldn't even sit down and sharpen his sword.

Blade was feeding the last munfans when Bairam came up behind him. The boy carried two swords, to mark his rank as Peython's son even though he was also a man under judgment for breaking the Law. "Hota will push himself forward every time he can," Bairam said. "He wants to be the hero of this journey, so he can ask our father for Kareena."

"Would Peython give her to him?"

"Hota's courage has won him many friends. If they spoke for him, Peython would have to listen, or fear them becoming his enemies."

"Kareena would not be happy with Hota, I think."

"No. I have heard her say she would rather marry an ox, or live without a man all her life."

Blade smiled, remembering Kareena's lips hot against him and her graceful red-brown body naked in the firelight. He doubted she would be happy with a celibate life, or would need to accept one, although he hoped she would not have to accept Hota just to keep peace in Kaldak. She would never be happy with a man who had more courage

56

than sense, even if he wasn't a loudmouthed boor as well.

It was well past noon before Hota and the other scouts returned. "There cannot be enough Doimari in Gilmarg to fight us," said Hota.

"Not unless they can hide themselves better than usual," added Sidas.

"The warriors of a city without the Law cannot have such skill," said Hota crushingly. Sidas was about to reply, but a black look from Kareena silenced him. Blade was glad. Sidas was too intelligent to believe much of Hota's superstitious nonsense about the Law, and much too likely to blurt out his heretical opinions in Hota's presence.

It was mid-afternoon before they got all the munfans un-tethered and on the move. They seemed more skittish than usual, and several broke their hobbles and tried to bolt. Even the most experienced hunters and munfan-leaders couldn't say what was bothering the animals.

The light was failing by the time they reached a safe refuge among the towers of Gilmarg, with a cracked roof overhead and crumbling vine-grown walls on three sides. Kareena decided against making any fires, and they ate a cold dinner of bread and meat. Then the sentries took up their posts for the night, and everyone else fell asleep.

Blade took the first watch with the sentries, then rolled up in his blanket. He managed to sleep in spite of the chill and the sharp rocks digging into all the more vulnerable portions of his anatomy. Sometime in the darkest hours of the night he awoke to find Kareena curled up against him, one arm across his chest. He tried to move her, but she only pressed herself closer without waking up and made a noise like a contented kitten. He gave up, wrapped his blanket around both of them, and went back to sleep with her firm warmth resting against him. Hota might be jealous, but Blade's patience with Hota was just about gone. If the warrior said one more word out of turn, Blade was going to find it hard not to take him apart, Law or no Law!

It didn't take them long the next morning to find Saorm's tunnel. Either the merchant had a naturally good memory, or knowing the number of swords pointed at his back gave him one. Before the sun was well up he'd led them through a maze of ruined side streets to a crumbling building with a half-exposed basement. In one corner of the basement stood a slab of concrete taller and thicker than a man.

"There," said Saorm. "Under the lower end of that stone. The tunnel is narrow, though. I did not get through it easily then. I do not think I could get through it at all, now."

Hota poked the merchant in his stomach. "Too fat, eh? We should have marched you harder, made you skinny. Well, there will always be *men* to go where you cannot."

At first Blade doubted that Saorm was telling the truth about pushing the slab into place single-handed. Then he noticed several other slabs balanced more or less precariously around the basement. One of them fell over as he watched, nearly crushing Sidas. When the dust settled, Kareena had the men go around and push the rest of the slabs over, so they could go to work on the tunnel without looking over their shoulders every minute.

One man might have pushed the slab into place, but it took the sweat of at least a dozen before it was clear. With Blade and Hota working together for once, the slab was then dragged to one side. Everyone stood around the gaping black maw now exposed, peering down the rubble-strewn slope until it vanished in the darkness. Blade noticed that while everyone wanted to look, no one seemed particularly eager to linger on the edge of the darkness.

To his credit, Saorm volunteerd to be the first man down the tunnel. He stripped himself naked, tied a rope around his waist, then on hands and knees scrambled down into the darkness. A lot of cursing and grunting and the clatter of falling stones floated up from the darkness, followed by a cloud of dust. Then Saorm himself reappeared, panting, sweaty, bleeding slightly in several places, and shaking his head grimly.

"The tunnel is not as it was when I found it. The stones have moved, so that there is much less room. Even if I was the man I was then, I could not get through."

Kareena gave him the kiss of honor. "Do not grieve,

Saorm. You have done well. Someone else will have to finish your work, that is all."

Kareena's words touched off a ferocious argument over who should have the honor of finishing Saorm's work. Blade was the first to volunteer to go down the tunnel. Inevitably, Hota objected. "This man is outside the Law and facing the judgment of the Gathering. It will bring a curse upon Kaldak if he is the first to enter the hole and see this great wealth of Oltec. Let *me* go." He looked ready to draw his sword against anyone who argued.

Saorm saw his chance to get back at Hota for his earlier insults. "You are larger than I, and the Law will not make you smaller. If I cannot get down, how can you?"

"Then Blade cannot go either, because he is bigger still."

"I am smaller than either of you," put in Sidas. "And I—"

"I am the smallest of the men," began Bairam. "I—"

"You may be Peython's son, but you are not in the Law's favor either," said Hota sharply. "You are not so much better than Blade."

"I am—*yah!*" said Bairam, breaking off as his sister kicked him hard in the shin. Kareena glared at everyone, then started taking off her trousers.

"*I* am the smallest of all. I am of Peython's blood. And no one can say that I am at fault before the Law. So I am the best one to go down, and no one will stop me."

When Kareena was naked, she bound her hair up, then let Blade tie the rope around her waist. When he'd done that, she picked up a rifle and vanished down the tunnel like a rabbit. They heard more curses and clatters and saw more clouds of dust. They also saw the rope vanishing steadily into the darkness. Then they heard Kareena's voice, distorted by the tunnel and by a spasm of coughing.

"I'm all the way—down. The fire jewels—by the Law, there must be *thousands* of them! Big stone in the tunnel, though. No one bigger than I—can get through. I'll try to move it."

"Be careful, Kareena," shouted Bairam. There was no reply, except more clattering stones. Dust poured out of the tunnel like smoke from a fire, and Blade started stripping off his own clothes. He might be the largest man in the

59

group, but he was also the strongest and the most skilled in this sort of work.

Then Kareena's voice came again, even more broken by coughing. "Can't—move—it. Almost—but somebody—push from above." She sounded as if she was about to strangle on the dust.

By now Blade was naked, wearing only his silver loinguard. Hota moved to block the tunnel, but Sidas and Bairam both stepped between him and Blade. Blade threw them both a look of gratitude, then got down on his hands and knees and started crawling. His natural caution over moving into the unknown fought with his desire to hurry to Kareena's rescue.

Stone by stone, Blade crept downward, the air growing thicker and the light fading with each foot he descended. He was in a weird sort of twilight by the time he came to what had to be the obstacle. It was another slab of concrete, tilted so that it left only about a two-foot space clear. Blade wondered how even Kareena could have slipped through, and hoped the stains on the slab were Saorm's blood and not hers.

Fortunately there was enough light to let Blade see how the slab could be moved out of the way. He crawled up onto the slab and shouted down into the darkness. "Kareena! Get out of the way. I'm going to be throwing the stones off the slab. Then you pull out the ones underneath."

A choking "Yes, Blade," from below reassured him that the girl was still alive and functioning. He started wrestling chunks of stone up over the lip of the slab and shoving them down into the lower part of the tunnel. As they crashed down, the dust rose about him until he was working more by touch then by sight, and he soon found himself coughing almost as hard as Kareena. Finally he'd cleared the top of the slab and scrambled back up to get a breath of fresh air and a crowbar.

It took Blade several tries before he found a position where he could pry up the slab without breaking either the crowbar or his back. Then he thrust the crowbar into place, waited until Kareena signaled she was ready, and heaved with all his strength.

Even Blade's powerful muscles nearly weren't enough. The slab was heavier than he'd expected. He had to lock muscles and joints, then press his back against the wall until he felt blood flow to keep holding it up. About all that kept him going was the knowledge that if he let the slab fall, it would squash Kareena like a cockroach.

Sweat oozed from every pore and his eyes nearly popped out of his head, but he held the slab long enough. Suddenly he heard Kareena's muffled, "All right, Blade. I'm safe." He jerked the bar free and the slab fell with a crash. The tunnel vanished completely in dust, and there were so many more rattles and crashes that for a horrible moment Blade was certain he'd brought the whole tunnel down on himself and Kareena. Then the noise died away and Blade clawed his way down the slope, through a gap now large enough to pass three men abreast.

He found Kareena sprawled on the floor, writhing and half-choking. She'd put the last of her strength into the effort, and if she didn't get out to the fresh air soon she was going to be in even worse condition. Blade opened his dust-clogged mouth to shout, but only a croak came out. Before he could get the breath to try again, there was another avalanche of small stones and Sidas, Bairam, and Hota came tumbling down the tunnel. Hota was carrying another crowbar, Sidas a torch and flint, and Bairam—bless him!—a leather skin full of water.

Bairam took one look at his sister, propped her up with one arm, and offered her the water. She vomited up the first mouthful, but kept down the second and third. After the fourth, she felt well enough to use some of the water to wipe her face. This left her with a sort of dark mask on her otherwise completely dust-coated skin. Like Blade, she was so thickly coated with dust that you had to look twice to see that she was naked.

Blade drank water until he no longer felt the dust grinding between his teeth. Then he lit the torch and slowly walked around the underground storeroom of the fire jewels. They were there as Saorm and Kareena said, thousands of them. No, tens of thousands, Blade corrected himself. There were crates which must contain at least a thousand of the smallest power cells, or a hundred of the larger ones.

There were covered racks of cells larger than any Blade had seen, and on the floor stood still more cells, each at least four feet high. If their power capacity was in proportion to their size, each of the big ones must hold enough power for a tank or even a small town! He was looking at nothing less than an Industrial Revolution for Kaldak, the saving of hundreds of lives and a whole generation on the road back to civilization . . .

Blade corrected himself again. He *could* be looking at all these things. He couldn't be sure, until he knew if most of these cells still held their power. Even after that, the Kaldakans would have to do some serious thinking about their Law before they could get the benefits of all this Oltec. Blade was sure there were far too many Kaldakans who would think like Hota, if you could call that "thinking" at all.

From the noise up above, it seemed that everyone in the expedition except the munfans wanted to come down the tunnel and stare at the Oltec. Kareena was now in shape to give orders again, and she kept everyone except Saorm and two men with rifles from coming down. "There is more Oltec here than we dreamed of," she shouted. "Who knows what the Sky Masters may have left behind to protect it? Until we know, the fewer down here the better."

Then, still naked, Kareena took one of the rifles. Slowly she raised it, and fumbled at the panel which covered the slot for the power cell. Saorm, Hota, and even Sidas stared horror-struck as she opened the panel and pulled out the old power cell. All eyes followed her as she stalked around the room, looking for the right size of power cell. She found an open crate, picked up a cell, blew the dust off, and held it up in the torchlight. It gleamed like new. By now even Blade was holding his breath.

Slowly, with trembling fingers, Kareena put the power cell in the rifle. It took her three tries before she could close the panel. She had to stop completely, her eyes closed and her breasts rising and falling, before she could raise the rifle.

Then in one smooth motion she raised it, aimed at the ceiling, and fired. The beam crackled across the room, dust and ozone stung Blade's nostrils, chips of hot stone stung his skin, and everything in sight turned a sickly green. He still felt like cheering. Some of the storeroom's Oltec lived!

"Then—we *can* make dead Oltec live?" said Sidas. He looked surprised half out of his wits.

"Yes," said Kareena. "The fire jewels are great Oltec. With their help—"

"You would destroy the Law?" grated Hota. He sounded like a rusty piece of machinery. "You, Peython's daughter? Then you must have his will for this—"

"We do have our father's will," said Bairam. "It is his will—"

Before Bairam could provoke a quarrel, Blade interrupted. The laser's light was brighter than anything from the torch. In the green glow he'd seen what appeared to be the head of a ladder in a far corner of the room. He took the torch from Saorm and led the merchant over to the corner.

He'd been right. The torch showed the top half-dozen rungs of a metal ladder, running down a circular metal shaft into the darkness. "Saorm, did you see this when you were here the first time?"

"Y-yes. I did."

"Did you climb down?"

Saorm looked horror-struck. "Blade, that would have been so far beyond the Law . . . !" He looked down at the blackness. "Also, I was afraid. Who knows what the Tower Builders left down there?"

Blade looked at the ladder reaching into nothingness and couldn't blame the man. "Who knows indeed?" he said. "I say nothing against you for that. But we must go down there now. We are already so far beyond the Law as it used to be, that there is no going back within it."

"For you, perhaps," said Hota. "But as for the rest of us, the Law—"

"Is not your own toy," said Bairam. It looked as if the quarrel Blade had hoped to prevent by calling attention to the ladder and the shaft was going to start after all.

Then a shrill scream floated down the tunnel and echoed horribly around the storeroom. Everyone with a weapon grabbed it. Another scream came from above, then in quick succession the crash of falling masonry, a heavy met-

63

allic thud, and the crackle of a laser much more powerful than any rifle.

Everyone made a rush for the tunnel at once and jammed in the entrance. As they struggled to get untangled, a third scream came, another laser-crackle, then the unmistakable odor of burning flesh. Then Blade finally heard coherent words coming from the tunnel entrance above.

"Help! Help! A giant is attacking us! An Oltec giant!"

Chapter 10

Blade could understand the words but still didn't know exactly what was happening. However, the cries, the laser fire, and the falling masonry said clearly enough that the people up on the surface were facing new danger.

Ruthlessly using feet and elbows, Blade got out of the tangle. He scrambled up the tunnel, more screams and laser fire echoing around him as he climbed. The smell of burning flesh grew stronger. As he hurled himself out of the mouth of the tunnel, the laser fire stopped and the metallic thuds came again.

As Blade stood up, he saw most of the people who'd been in the room vanishing up the stairs to the second floor. One lay on the floor, writhing silently, too horribly burned to be able to scream. Two others crouched in a corner, a man and a woman with their arms around each other. A moment later Blade heard an appalling crash. Cracks appeard in the wall to the right of the door to the street. *Crash, crash, crash!* A section of wall twice as high as a man disintegrated and came down in a pile of fragments and a cloud of dust. Through the hole Blade caught a glimpse of something moving—then a laser burned a yard-wide gap in the stairs. At the same time the breeze outside swept away the veil of dust. At last Blade had a good look at the Oltec "giant." He threw himself on the floor behind the largest piece of rubble he could find, as another laser blast deepened the crater in the stairs.

The giant was a humanoid robot at least twelve feet tall. Its slab-sided rectangular body was mounted on two massive legs with armored knee and ankle joints. Two equally massive arms with armored elbows and hands with four jointed fingers were tearing chunks out of the wall. In the middle of the chest glowed the laser tube.

The head was a grotesque parody of a World War II German helmet, with eyes, a mouth, and ears. The "eyes" were obviously some sort of scanner, although one was cracked and dark. The "mouth" was the black tubular muzzle of what looked like another weapon. The "ears" were sound receptors or possibly radio receivers; one of them had a long antenna trailing from it. The whole robot was a silvery brown—once this might have been a finish designed to reflect laser beams. Now it seemed tarnished and worn from many years of neglect and many battles.

The two Kaldakans in the corner now sprang up and made a dash for the stairs. The woman hesitated on the lip of the smoking gap in the stairs, giving the robot an easy shot at her. A laser beam cut her in two before she could scream. Her torso and head dropped into the crater, while her legs rolled back down the stairs.

The man howled like a wild animal. He leaped the crater safely, then turned and fired at the robot. It was a wild shot, hitting the robot in one knee and doing no harm. The robot lifted in one hand a chunk of wall the size of a man's head and flung it with horrible precision. The Kaldakan fell backward into the crater, his chest a crushed red mess.

Blade frowned. The war robot was obviously a creation of the Sky Masters, and therefore centuries old. It was still formidable enough to wipe out the whole Kaldakan expedition if it wasn't led away and destroyed. That was a job Blade knew he'd have to face single-handed. Some of the Kaldakans were fast and quick-witted, but none of them had the understanding of modern technology needed to give them the right reactions. The Law had suppressed their curiosity for too long.

Blade mentally damned the Law and looked at the robot again. The hole in the wall was now large enough to let it come into the room, but it seemed to be hesitating. Perhaps it was programmed not to walk on floors which might be unable to support its weight. The thing must weigh two or three tons!

However, it wasn't going to stand there making up its mind forever. Blade crawled to the mouth of the tunnel and called down, hoping the robot's "hearing" was impaired with age. "Kareena! Keep everyone down there until someone tells you it's safe. There's an Oltec war machine up here that's gone mad with age. I've got to lead it away from here, then destroy it." He hoped she would understand what she had to do from this brief explanation.

He heard Kareena's muffled voice agreeing, then heard her cursing. After that came the scrabbling and rattle of someone climbing rapidly up the tunnel. A moment later Saorm popped out, pale and sweating but carrying two laser rifles and a bulky leather sack over one shoulder.

"What—?" began Blade, but Saorm only handed him a rifle, pointed at the bag, and whispered:

"Fire jewels. For the Oltec."

Blade nodded. Extra power cells for the rifles would be useful, although he doubted if rifle fire would be enough for the robot. It had to be armored against much heavier weapons.

However, there could still be uses for the rifles. Blade took a fresh power cell, loaded it into his rifle, then aimed it at a far corner of the room and let fly. The cracked and shaken wall started to shed more fragments and dust. The robot's head slowly turned, and its own laser stabbed into the same corner. The corner erupted in dusty and flying debris, then the wall collapsed completely and took part of the floor above with it. The roar of collapsing masonry completely drowned out Blade's and Saorm's footsteps as they sprinted across the room and up the stairs. The fog of dust filling the room was thick enough to hide them completely.

Once around the bend in the stairs, the merchant leaned against the wall to catch his breath. "Thank you, Saorm," said Blade. "You've done well. Now stay here while I—"

Saorm shook his head. "I am not going to leave your back bare or your Oltec dead."

"You are no warrior, Saorm. Forgive me for sounding like Hota, but—"

"I am the father of Geyrna, who has caught the eye of a warrior who is my chief's son. Peython will judge the father's worth as well as the daughter's, when it comes time to choose a wife for his son."

"You have already—"

"I have *not* done enough, Blade. And can you truly say that having a comrade will make no difference in this battle against the war Oltec?"

Blade couldn't. He would rather have had Sidas or Kareena at his side, of course. But they were trapped in the storeroom—possibly trapped for good if he didn't draw the robot off fairly soon. If Saorm was this determined, there was no point in wasting precious time by arguing.

Besides Sidas knew Gilmarg much better than he did. That could turn out to be important.

"All right," said Blade, not trying to conceal his irritation. "But if you get tired or are wounded, I'll have to leave you behind. I'll come back for you if I live, but I can't wait for you."

"That is the way of war, Blade. Even a merchant knows that much."

Blade mentally threw up his hands in resignation and led the way up the stairs to where the other Kaldakans were hiding. Since he saw none of the natural leaders up here, he spoke to all of them. He had to choose his words carefully, to tell them what to do without revealing so much knowledge of Oltec that anyone would become suspicious of him.

"This is a machine of the Sky Masters, made for war. It has gone mad with age, so it must be destroyed. I have more of the knowledge needed to do this than anyone of Kaldak. It does not matter that I am outside the Law, for this machine is also outside the Law.

"So I will take the machine away from here and find a

67

way to destroy it. When it is gone, go down to the room below and bring up the people in the tunnel. Help them also bring up all the fire jewels everyone can carry. Then leave the city at once. Do not try to save the munfans. That will draw the robot on to you like a greathawk on to a lamb. You must save yourselves first."

Blade saw a few faces still blank with surprise or fear. Most seemed to understand what he was proposing and didn't resent taking advice from a man outside the Law as long as he was the only one with some idea of what to do. He turned to Saorm.

"All right. Let's go play bait."

Blade and Saorm climbed down the vines from a rear window on the second floor. Then they hurried around to the front, to find the robot still standing there. It couldn't get into the building and its enemies wouldn't come out. So Blade and Saorm took cover half a block up the street, then opened fire with their rifles.

Instantly the robot turned its head, its body followed the head around with surprising speed, and the laser chewed a piece out of the wall above the two men. A fragment large enough to crush Blade's skull came close enough to part his hair. Before the robot could fire again, Blade and Saorm were running up the street. Both hoped it would follow. After a moment's hesitation, it did. In fact it came after them so fast that Blade looked back to find it gaining on them rapidly. They were both zigzagging, but in another minute it would be too close for safety.

"To the right!" Saorm followed Blade's gesture and darted down a sidestreet with the Englishman at his heels. The robot saw them turning but fired too late. A section of the corner building two stories high crashed down and spread itself across the street in smoking rubble. More of the building was tottering. Blade stopped in the shelter of a doorway, hoping to see the robot come close enough to be caught by the next fall of masonry.

Instead it gave the building a wide berth. When the collapse did come the robot was already well out of danger and advancing on Blade. As it marched out of the cloud of dust and smoke, its laser fired again. A chunk of pavement

flew up like a soccer ball, crashed into the front of a building just ahead of Blade, and brought down several large
pieces of metal facing. Blade and Saorm barely jumped
aside in time, and Blade was now painfully aware that two
could play this game of dropping buildings on the enemy.
He decided to keep to the main streets as much as possible
and use the side streets only for cover. The robot could
turn so well that there was no reason to try leading it
around sharp corners and hope it would fall or crash into a
building.

Blade and Saorm headed west as fast as they could,
nearly getting lost several times but usually drawing the
robot after them. Twice it seemed to lose track of them,
and once Blade saw it turn back toward the east. Assuming
it was turning back toward the Kaldakans, he opened fire,
was nearly killed by the robot's laser, but at least got its
attention again.

Blade wondered why the laser was fixed in the robot's
chest rather than mounted in the swiveling head. He could
only guess that the black muzzle in the head was some sort
of close-range weapon, perhaps a grenade launcher. He
hoped it was empty. A few grenades could have finished
the Kaldakans, and one lucky shot could do the job on him
and Saorm. On the other hand, lasers worked only on line-
of-sight. You couldn't fire them in a curve over anything
or through anything too solid.

Of course this worked both ways. Blade and Saorm had
to expose themselves to fire at the robot. They were
smaller targets, but they were much more vulnerable.
There didn't seem to be any part of the robot they could
hurt with the rifles, at least before the robot could bring its
own heavier weapon to bear. Blade quickly knew that he
and Saorm were going to have to win by skill rather than
by strength.

Several times Blade tried to lead the robot across the
bridges over Gilmarg's numerous canals, hoping its weight
would collapse a bridge under it. Each time the robot
stopped at the head of the bridge. Each time Blade had to
recross the canal before he could get the robot moving
again. He hoped the Kaldakans were on their way out of

the city by now, but he couldn't be sure. At least he hadn't heard any laser fire from the east, so the robot was probably operating alone.

Blade did notice that when the robot turned its head, its feet sometimes kept going for several more steps in the old direction. This happened often enough to make Blade wonder if the robot's computer "brain" was slightly defective. After all these years it very well might be, and this could give him and Saorm an opening. There should be places where the banks of the canals which criss-crossed Gilmarg were so overgrown with foliage that they were hidden. If they led the robot straight toward one of those places, then suddenly drew its attention to one side, the robot's legs would continue to take it forward a few more steps, and then . . .

They were far enough ahead of the robot now so that Blade could lead Saorm into a doorway and force him to sit down for a minute. The merchant was gasping for breath.

"I'll need you for our next trick," said Blade. "But if that doesn't work, I want you to give up this chase."

"My honor—my daughter—I'm just a bit short—of—breath."

"You'll drop dead if you go on much longer," said Blade sharply. "I'd rather bring you home to Geyrna than tell her how gallantly you died! Now, is there a place where the canal bank is so overgrown that the robot might not see it until too late?"

There was, and Saorm led Blade toward it as quickly as the robot would let them go. They could never forget the searing green death licking at their heels, and Blade was beginning to worry. Saorm really did look ready to fall over, and he himself wasn't going to be able to play hide and seek with this mechanical monster forever. Human flesh could not compete with steel and electricity in an endurance contest.

Then they were out on the bank high above the canal and trotting rapidly along the street toward the park where Saorm had said there would be a good place to set their trap. As the robot turned onto the street half a mile behind them, Blade saw something peculiar about the pavement ahead. For fifty yards the pavement slabs of the street were tilted slightly toward the canal. Blade looked across the canal. There were actually *two* streets, an upper and a lower roadway one above the other, supported by the steel columns. He then looked over the railing along the street on his side of the canal. It was the same on this side. Those shaky pavement blocks ahead hid a fifteen-foot drop to the roadway below.

That should be enough, and suddenly Blade had a different plan. The trap in the park forgotten for the moment, Blade quickly gave Saorm his instructions, conscious of the robot tramping steadily toward them. The merchant staggered off toward the next bridge, his eyes so glazed with fatigue Blade wondered if he could even see the robot, let alone hit it. Well, with luck he wouldn't need to hit it to draw its attention.

Then the robot was within range and Blade began his dance of death with it. He darted back and forth across the street high above the canal, never stopping even to fire his rifle, always watching the robot, always seeing it tramp steadily forward, firing every few yards. He began to fear it would step on one of the loose slabs and spring the trap prematurely.

Now the robot needed only about ten more steps before it reached the loose slabs. "Fire," Blade whispered to Saorm. "Fire!" He wanted to scream, but his throat felt as if someone was firing a miniature laser inside it. His chest felt as tight as if the robot was already gripping him in one hand.

"Fire!"

Green light speared out from a window on the far side of the canal. The robot's head swiveled to scan the direction of the new attack, while its feet took the last few steps onto the first of the loose blocks.

For a moment Blade couldn't be sure his trick had worked. Then several tons of robot made the slab give up its long struggle against the force of gravity. Instead of tilting toward the canal, the slab tilted toward the buildings inland. It tilted so slowly that for another moment Blade thought the robot might have time to step backward. The robot stopped, sensed that something was wrong, and lifted

71

a foot for a backward step. Then the slab cracked completely in two, and the robot vanished as if it had fallen through a trapdoor.

Blade was running toward the hole before the echoes of the robot's fall died. He approached the hole from the rear to avoid the laser but quickly saw he needn't have bothered. The robot's chest was crushed against a steel column, and the laser was sizzling and sputtering like all the frying pans in the world put together. Acrid gas poured up past Blade, and sparks and bits of molten metal dripped down into the water from the lower roadway. Blade sighted in on the robot's neck and fired his rifle. He kept firing until the rifle was too hot to hold. He let it cool off, then started firing again until the power cell was completely dead. By then half the robot's neck was black and distorted, and clouds of foul-smelling smoke told Blade of burned-out circuitry. By the time Saorm staggered up with the other rifle, Blade was sure the robot was helpless if not permanently wrecked.

He clapped the merchant on the back. "Saorm, I don't know what the Law says, or what the Law says *I* can say. But I say here and now—this day you've been a warrior and a friend. Let no one say a word against Geyrna's father in *my* presence."

"Thank you, Blade. I—" Suddenly he went down on hands and knees, started shaking all over, then vomited into the hole. Blade let him alone. Tougher men than Saorm could have got the shakes after this weird battle. As long as he'd waited until after the fight, it was all right.

Finally Saorm rose, wiped his mouth, and looked down at the robot. "So we've won."

"We've won today's battle," said Blade. "But I suspect it was only the first battle in what could be a very long war."

"The Law spare us that!" exclaimed Saorm.

Blade shook his head. "I do not think the Law will make much difference one way or another. In fact, I would say that today saw the end of Kaldak of the Law."

Chapter 11

Blade examined the robot quickly, ignoring the danger of booby traps. He wanted the job done before either new enemies or the Kaldakans arrived. By the time he'd finished, he was even more sure than before that nothing would ever be the same again in this Dimension. Strictly speaking, the fallen machine was not a robot, a self-contained mechanical imitation of a human being. Instead it was controlled from a distance by a computer or possibly a human operator, getting commands by radio and sending back visual and sound information from its sensors. In spite of its humanoid form, it reminded Blade of the remote-controlled waldoes in Home Dimension used for handling radioactive materials. Now if he could just find a way to disable or jam the radio equipment . . .

That hope soon vanished. The radio equipment was so sophisticated and apparently so nearly indestructible that Blade couldn't have figured out a way of defeating it with all the resources of Home Dimension technology available. Lord Leighton might have been able to improvise something, but Blade wasn't that kind of electronics expert.

Blade's grim look seemed to depress Saorm even more. The merchant was sitting on the edge of the hole, staring at nothing. It seemed he couldn't face the idea of a Kaldak totally without the Law.

"Blade, Blade," he moaned. "If there is no Law, what will become of my daughter, who has already given herself to Bairam? Without the Law, how will he think of her?"

"He'll think of her as his bride, or at least a woman to be

well treated. If the Law doesn't tell him that, my fist will," said Blade. "I think Peython and Kareena will help me too."

The idea that the passing of the Law would not necessarily bring dishonor to his daughter seemed to cheer up Saorm. He rose and began in a fumbling way to study the two laser rifles.

He was still at work when the rest of the expedition came up on foot, with Kareena in the lead. When she saw Blade standing unharmed, she gave a wordless little cry and ran to him, ignoring Hota's black look.

"Blade! Are you all right? We thought—"

"You were wrong," said Blade wearily. He was too tired and too conscious of the need for haste to be polite. "I am all right. Are the munfans ready to go?"

"Yes. But must we leave so soon, when there is so much new Oltec to learn?"

She had a point. There ought to be some alternative to a headlong retreat, waldoes or no waldoes. However, they couldn't really afford to risk losing what they'd already gained in the hope of winning more. He explained the situation.

"So the Oltec machine had to be sent by men?" asked Sidas when Blade was finished. "Is it possible that—the Tower Builders still live somewhere in the land?"

Blade shook his head. "If the Tower Builders still lived, there would have been other signs of them long before now. Also, this war machine would not have gone mad. I think someone in a city has learned how to use these machines and is sending them against his enemies."

"The Doimari!" growled Bairam. He cursed. "They have always lived under a weak Law. Now instead of being cursed, they find *these* to sweep the land."

"We shall not keep the Doimari from sweeping the Land by throwing aside the Law ourselves," said Hota firmly. "So before we do anything else, let us all take new oaths to the Law."

"Before we do anything else," said Kareena, "we shall let Blade of England finish what he has to say."

"A man outside the Law?"

"A man who has beaten an enemy not even you could

have fought. You are not outside the Law, Hota, but you will be outside my favor if you speak again before Blade has finished."

It was probably just as well that no one heard what Hota muttered under his breath while everyone else was listening to Blade. "The rest of you should load the munfans with all the fire jewels they can carry and return to Kaldak as fast as you can. Then you should begin to search Kaldak for underground rooms with fire jewels and other Oltec which you can use against the machines."

"What about you, Blade?" asked Sidas.

"I will stay behind in Gilmarg," he said. "I want to look for more Oltec. I will start with what may lie at the bottom of the ladder in the room of the fire jewels. Though I am outside the Law, I know more about what to seek. I can fight or run better than anyone else if the Doimari send more Oltec machines."

"Yes," someone said, "but since you *are* outside the Law, you should not be left alone with all this Oltec. Someone within the Law must stay with you."

"I can stay with you," said Saorm. He had his color back now and was standing with a rifle over his shoulder. He looked like a self-confident combat veteran.

"No," said Blade. "You were very valiant during the fight with the war machine, but I don't think you'd live through another such encounter. No, you must return to the city and help in the search there."

Everyone seemed to be trying to look at everyone else at once. Although no one quite wanted to leave Blade alone in Gilmarg, no one was eager to volunteer to face Doimari, waldoes, and the Sky Masters alone knew what else. Blade was relieved to see that at least neither Bairam nor Hota had volunteered.

Sidas seemed about to speak, then Kareena stamped her foot. "Are none of you *men*? Then *I* will stay behind with Blade. No one can say that I am not within the Law."

"So, you're finally going to let Blade bed you?" said Hota. He spoke loudly enough to be overheard but not so loud that anyone who wanted to ignore him couldn't do so. Blade saw Kareena silently grit her teeth and hoped Bairam would have the sense to do the same.

Instead Bairam drew his sword so violently that he nearly dropped it, then stepped toward Hota. Kareena tried to hold him back, but he shook off her hand fiercely.

"Hota, you will eat those words."

Hota's own sword rasped out of its scabbard. "You will eat my sword long before that, Bairam. You may be of Peython's blood, but I begin to wonder. Would Peython have a son ready to sell his sister to someone outside the Law?"

At this point Blade would cheerfully have strangled Bairam with his bare hands. From the look on Kareena's face she would probably have helped him. However, there was Hota to deal with first. Everyone else was hovering around the two swordsmen, not knowing whether they should back off and give them room to fight or try to break up the duel. Custom and the Law said the duel should be fought. Common sense said it should be stopped. Then Blade pushed his way through the circle and stepped up to Hota.

"Hota, I say that you are a coward, to fight Bairam who has not your strength. I say that you will prove anything only by fighting me to the death."

Hota spat at Blade's feet. "You are outside the Law, Blade. Now stand out of the way."

"So are you, Hota. The Law is made for men. You are much less of a man than Kareena. You are only an animal who talks too much and foolishly. I say this, and I will go on saying it while I live. So kill me or hear it from me every day while I am in Kaldak."

Hota's scream really was more like an animal's cry than anything human. Blade jumped back as Hota's sword flashed past his chest three times, in three savage thrusts. Then several men gripped Hota's arms and shoulders, pulling him back. He screamed and cursed until Blade was afraid the men holding him would have to knock him out. Blade very much wanted the fight to go to a conclusion.

"Hota, will you prove Blade's words the truth?" said Sidas angrily. "Does a brave man fight with a sword against bare hands?"

Blade laughed. "Do not take his sword from him, Sidas.

76

In England we have ways of fighting with our bare hands which you do not have in the Land. So Hota with his sword and me with my hands is a fair fight, as long as neither of us is wearing armor. Hota, I will fight as I stand if you will meet me—"

"I will, by the Law! Now let me go, you—!"

Reluctantly, Sidas and the others let Hota go. He shook himself to loosen his muscles, then raised his sword and sprang forward. Blade dropped into unarmed-combat stance and hoped this gamble would pay off. Facing Hota with his bare hands would give him a perfect excuse for killing the man, and Hota had to die. With his loud mouth, his bigotry about the Law, and his many friends among the warriors, he'd simply become too dangerous to be left alive. Blade was going to have to terminate him, as cold-bloodedly as he'd ever terminated a KGB agent. In fact there'd been KGB agents he'd killed with more regrets than he would feel in Hota's case. On the other hand, bare hands against bare steel *was* a gamble. Blade was confident of his skill in unarmed combat, but he was also aware of Hota's speed and strength. If the man was able to slow Blade down at all, this fight might have a very ugly ending.

Blade quickly discovered that Hota's combination of speed and a short sword gave the man a nearly perfect defense. If he'd been using a longer sword which he had to raise before striking, Blade might have been able to get in under it. As it was, he found the sword's point darting at his ribs every time he tried to close. If it got to be a life-or-death matter, he could always take the sword in his shoulder, immobilizing Hota's weapon. Then he could strike with his free hand. He didn't want to do that yet, though. Gilmarg had to be explored, and he'd be damned if he was going to try exploring it with one arm out of action!

So Blade kept his distance as much as he could without looking too cautious. Several times he managed to get in a kick at Hota's hip from the man's left. This slowed Hota down a little but not much. After the fourth kick he started guarding with his left arm held low. The next time Blade kicked, Hota's hand clamped down on Blade's ankle like the claw of the waldo. Blade had to kick, twist, and roll all in one motion to get free without being run through. Even then Hota's sword gashed the back of his leg.

As he got up, Blade heard Kareena gasp with relief and close her eyes. He wished she'd keep herself more under control. Knowing that Kareena was on Blade's side could drive Hota into a berserk attack, caring nothing about his survival as long as he could take Blade with him.

Fortunately the cut was shallow. In Home Dimension a light bandage would have been enough for it. He wasn't even going to lose any speed. Just as well, since Hota seemed to be a more intelligent fighter than he'd expected.

Suddenly Blade realized that the way Hota reacted to Blade's kicks opened a possible line of attack. Blade feinted twice with his kicks and saw Hota make the same response each time. *Not so intelligent after all*, Blade thought. *Putting both arms in predictable positions isn't a good idea in a fight.* Blade decided to make his move the next time. Otherwise Hota might get suspicious, and he himself was going to be losing speed from sheer fatigue before much longer. Hota hadn't been chased all over Gilmarg by a runaway waldo!

Blade closed, then stood with one leg loose, the other stiffened. Hota gave his war cry and thrust fiercely at Blade's exposed and immobile stomach. Blade wheeled on his stiffened leg and brought the edge of his left hand across the side of Hota's neck. At the same time he folded to the right and gripped Hota's wrist. The sword point darted past Blade, inches away from castrating him. All of Hota's forward motion was now a free gift to Blade.

With that help, Blade's strength and his grip on Hota's shoulder and arm easily did the rest. In a single smooth motion Blade dropped and Hota rose. The Kaldakan let out a scream as he found himself in midair, then hit the ground headfirst with a gruesome crunch. Blade stepped back, noting that Hota's skull was flattened on top and his whole head was at an impossible angle to his shoulders.

Then Kareena was in Blade's arms, and this time he didn't even want to push her away. He wasn't feeling quite so cold-blooded now that Hota was dead, and it helped not to have to look at the man's body for a while.

Finally Kareena stepped away from Blade and turned to the others. "You see that Hota is dead, from the bare hands of a man he fought with a sword. A man he said was outside the Law! I say that if Blade is outside the Law, then the Law itself is not as it should be." Several people flinched at those words, but nobody dared say anything. Blade himself wouldn't have argued with Kareena, not when she had her sword drawn and looked ready to kill anyone who argued.

"I will stay here in Gilmarg with Blade, and we shall study the secrets of the Tower Builders. Whatever we do or leave undone will be for the good of Kaldak, in the war which is coming. The rest of you, start loading the munfans!"

Bairam stepped forward. "My sister, our chief's daughter, speaks well. My sword will go where she or Blade of England tells it to go."

"Mine likewise," said Sidas.

"And mine."

"Mine, also."

"Yes. A new time has come for Kaldak."

And so on, until nearly everyone had sworn to obey Kareena and Blade. No doubt they were taking his victory over Hota as an omen. Blade felt more relieved than proud. Knowing which orders to give was always important, but being able to get them obeyed was even more so.

Chapter 12

At dawn the next day Blade and Kareena stood side by side in an upper-floor window on the edge of Gilmarg. Far across the fields they saw the last munfans tramping toward the forest. Green light flickered three times from behind the munfans.

"That's Sidas signaling farewell," said Blade. "Now it's up to us."

"Do you think they'll have enough fire—I mean, power cells?"

"They've got all we could hope to get out of Gilmarg without waiting for the Doimari to strike again," said Blade. "Thanks to Sidas, that's many more than I'd hoped."

Sidas had made a suggestion so sensible that Blade was embarrassed he hadn't thought of it himself. For a short distance a munfan could carry three or four times its normal load. So why not load the munfans until they could barely walk, lead them to the forest, unload them, bring them back, and repeat the whole process all night. It didn't matter if the power cells got all the way to Kaldak at once, as long as they were out of Gilmarg before any more Doimari came. The Doimari seldom came into the forests, and even if they did you could hide a whole city under the trees, never mind a pile of Oltec!

Sidas, Blade decided, was going to be an extremely useful man in the new Kaldak with its new Law. Once he was convinced it was possible to do something at all, he would think very clearly about how to do it. Blade had told Bairam, "If Kareena and I don't come back, be sure Sidas gets the honor he deserves. Listen to him yourself, too. He thinks before he speaks."

Bairam had flushed. "And I still do not?"

Blade had clapped Bairam on the shoulder. "You're getting better. But you still have a long way to go."

"I know." He had sighed. "And you have made it even longer than it was before you came. I hope you stay a long time, Blade. Even my father could not do all which must be done to help Kaldak go where it must . . ."

"Blade," Kareena now said insistently, breaking into his thoughts. "Will they have enough power cells to fight a war against Doimar?"

"I don't think they'll have to fight the whole war with what they have now," said Blade. "There was a storeroom full of power cells under Gilmarg, in spite of all the years

80

the Doimari have been coming to it. Why shouldn't there be some under Kaldak, when you've never even looked for them?"

Kareena smiled and turned away from the window. "True. Who knows what lies in the darkness beyond the Law? Shall we go down and look?"

"—one hundred fifty-two. One hundred fifty-three. One hundred fifty-four. One hundred fifty-five."

Blade listened to Kareena's voice counting the rungs of the ladder, then looked down. Twenty feet below, the lantern, dangling from a rope around his waist, made a flickering, unsteady ring of orange light on the walls of the shaft. He saw no sign of any opening or even a closed door.

How far down did this shaft go? With one hundred sixty rungs at a foot and a half each, they were already two hundred and forty feet below the level of the storeroom, and that was already a good fifty feet below ground level. They were already half again as deep as the Dimension X complex under the Tower of London, and with no elevator.

At least there was no elevator now. Once there must have been some sort of machinery for lifting equipment, if not people. Anything worth burying this far underground must have held items which couldn't be hauled up and down a ladder on people's backs. Perhaps this particular shaft was for ventilation and used by people only in an emergency. In that case the main shaft for whatever lay below must be elsewhere. Blade didn't like the idea of searching an underground maze for an elevator which probably no longer worked. On the other hand, he liked even less the thought of climbing back up this shaft rung by rung, with the Doimari quite possibly waiting at the top.

He stopped and flexed the kinks out of each arm and leg in turn. The lantern below swung through a wider arc, nearly striking the wall. As it steadied, Blade saw an unfamiliar pattern on the wall at the very edge of the light. He quickly descended four more rungs and looked again. The pattern was like bars or wire mesh over a large opening. Another five rungs downward, and Blade was sure.

It was an opening, large enough for a man, but it was also blocked by a door of metal bars as thick as Blade's thumb. Blade reeled in the lantern, hung it on a rung, then unslung his rifle and prepared to fire it.

"Won't that kill it?" Kareena asked.

"Remember the power cells. If it dies, we can make it live again."

Kareena shook her head in irritation at her own mistake. "I am sorry, Blade. I am not used to thinking of how life goes, when we are so far beyond the Law as I have known it." She hesitated. "Blade, do all the men of England think beyond the Law as easily as you do?"

"No," said Blade shortly. That wasn't a line of questioning he wanted her to follow very far. He aimed the rifle at the nearest corner of the door and pulled the trigger. The shaft lit up with the familiar green laser glow. Even though the glow reached much farther than the lantern's light Blade saw no bottom to the shaft.

It took a complete power cell and part of another before the door was cut loose. The dark metal of the bars was nearly as tough as the silvery Englor alloy of Blade's loinguard. He waited until the bars cooled off a little, used the muzzle of his rifle to swing the gate open, and waited a little while longer. Even an emergency exit might have electronic sentinels if what lay beyond it was important enough. Some of these sentinels might even have survived the centuries since the fall of the Tower Builders.

The darkness beyond the doorway gave back nothing but silence. Finally Blade swung himself into the door, then helped Kareena down. They stood together on the edge of the unknown for a moment, Kareena's arm stealing around Blade's waist. Then Blade laughed loud enough to raise echoes and struck a dramatic pose, holding the lantern high.

"Forward! To the future of Kaldak!"

He'd hit the proper note. Kareena also laughed and stepped away from him. Side by side they walked into the darkness.

Directly ahead of them lay a single long corridor, with a metal floor and stone walls sprayed with some sort of plastic. The plastic was cream-colored and the floor a tarnished green. A translucent strip ran down the middle of the ceiling, probably the lighting system. At irregular intervals plain steel doors were set in the walls. The first three Blade tried were solidly locked.

"Why can't you burn a way through them?" asked Kareena, when they'd left the third door behind.

"Because they're too thick," said Blade. "I would use up too much of our power. Also, we don't know what's inside those doors. It might catch fire or explode." To emphasize his words he thumped the fourth door with his fist. It resounded as dully as the others, but then swung open several inches. Kareena giggled. Blade put his shoulder to the door and pushed with unnecessary vigor. It flew open so violently it crashed against the stone wall inside.

The lantern showed rack after rack of crates, cans, boxes, and man-high cylinders all around the room. In the middle was a table, piled on one end with small cylindrical cans with spray buttons on the tops. An overturned chair lay on the far side. Blade started walking around the room, holding the lantern up to each rack. Either the language of the Tower Builders was very different from that of their descendants, or the containers were marked in some sort of code. Blade couldn't understand more than one word or sign in ten on any of the labels. Finding out what was inside the containers was going to be a matter of trial and error. Not the best way, when one error could be fatal.

A clatter and an exclamation from Kareena made Blade turn around. She'd brushed against the table, knocking several of the metal cans off onto the floor. Blade sniffed. There was a faint smell in the air which hadn't been there before, rather like a cheap perfume.

"There's still something in the cans, Blade," said Kareena. Before he could stop her she picked up one and pressed the button down on one end. There was a faint hissing and the perfume smell grew stronger. "It smells like a kind of soap," she said merrily.

"Kareena—!"

She stretched out one bare arm, aimed the can at it, and pressed the spray button again. A patch of skin turned wet and glistening. Then Blade grabbed the can and snatched it out of her hand. "Kareena, you don't know what that is! It could be a poison, even if it smells like perfume!"

But Kareena was too busy rubbing the sprayed patch of

skin to listen. "Blade it *is* a kind of soap," she said finally. "Look." Blade had to admit that the patch of skin she'd sprayed was much cleaner than it had been, and showed no sign of damage. "A liquid soap in a can! We've never found anything like that! What else do you suppose we're going to find?" She sounded like a child anticipating a visit to the toy store.

Blade didn't want to quarrel with Kareena. He also didn't want her kittenish curiosity to kill them both. "I do not know," he said. "The Oltec the Sky Masters left here in the Land is different from what they left in England. I do know that we must be very careful. So never, *never* play with anything you find the way you did now. You were very foolish and very lucky."

Kareena's eyes went hard and for a moment Blade was sure a quarrel was about to start. Then she sighed. "Blade, I suppose you are right. I did not think. I am not used to living so far beyond the Law that one must think about this sort of thing."

"True, and so must everyone else in Kaldak. You're all going to have to learn."

"Yes, but if we don't play with what we find, how are we going to learn anything about it?" She gestured around the room. "There must be enough new Oltec here to keep fifty people busy learning about it."

"Then we'll come back with fifty people, and they can go to work. That way if one man makes a mistake and gets killed, the other forty-nine can see what happened and learn from it. If *we* get killed, all we've learned dies with us. It may never get back to Kaldak at all and certainly won't get back in time to help against the Doimari."

"You think there is really going to be a war?"

"You saw that machine, Kareena. If Kaldak had a hundred of them, wouldn't your father be tempted to try destroying Doimar. And he is a man who prefers peace and the Law. I have not heard that Feragga of Doimar is fond of either." That was a considerable understatement. From what he'd heard of the woman who ruled Doimar, she was something to frighten naughty children with at bedtime!

Kareena nodded reluctantly. "Very well, Blade. I will

84

follow where you lead." Blade noticed that this promise didn't keep her from scooping three cans of the spray soap into her pack.

Blade led on, trying to look more sure of where he was going than he actually was. His confidence grew as he found that about half the rooms were unlocked. After the third open room he was no longer leading quite so much in the dark. One rack there held several dozen portable lamps as powerful as miniature searchlights. They lit up the whole main corridor and showed a number of side ones as well. Blade refused to worry now about triggering alarms or defenses. He and Kareena were already far enough inside the complex to be helpless if any defenses *did* go into action. They were also far enough inside to have triggered them off a dozen times if they still worked.

Blade counted about forty rooms in the complex. Some of the open ones were empty or used only for what had to be junk. In many of the filled ones everything was so tightly packaged or sealed that Blade was reluctant to disturb it. He still found enough on display to impress him.

There were hundreds of sets of infantry equipment, including uniforms, boots, gas masks, body armor, and weapons. There were other garments which looked like radiation or chemical protection for rescue workers. There were portable radios and miniature computers. There was enough medical equipment for a small army, including what seemed to be a complete portable operating room. There were tons of rations, some still edible after all the years lying in the darkness. There were no waldoes or any vehicles except a few small freight trucks, but there was everything else needed to help the people of a bombed city defend its ruins.

Kareena was too amazed at the richness of the Oltec to say anything more for quite a while. When she could finally speak, the first thing she asked was, "Do you suppose there's something like this under Kaldak?"

Blade nodded. "It would make sense to have supplies stored under each city. It might be hard to carry them from one city to another in the middle of a war."

"Then—all we had to do, to be as strong as Doimar— was to go a little farther down in Kaldak than the Law said we could? Then—it is because we have obeyed the Law that Kaldak has been put in danger?"

She looked and sounded so confused that Blade wished he could soften his answer, but knew he could not. "Yes. That is so. And the first thing we do when we return to Kaldak is explore every basement and every hole in every basement in the city."

They moved on, collecting samples of the smaller items as they went. Although they tried to restrain themselves, by the time they reached the center of the complex their packs were bulging and so heavy they were glad to unsling them for a while.

The center of the complex was unmistakably a command center of some sort. There was a central room with consoles, displays, and screens on all four sides. There were six reclining couches, and four unidentifiable contraptions with seats, helmets, gloves, and boots all wired to massive metal frames. Blade wondered if they were communications devices, or perhaps equipment for interrogating (and torturing) prisoners.

The rest of the command center included two bunkrooms, a storeroom full of rations and uniforms, and a bathroom. Kareena peered into the bathroom, grinned, then flexed cramped shoulder muscles. "Blade, I think I'm going to take the first bath anyone's taken here since the fall of the Sky Masters."

"I doubt if the water's running," said Blade, smiling.

Kareena sat down on the floor and started pulling off her boots. "Remember that soap-water in the cans? There should be some more in the storeroom."

There was. Blade brought four cans of it, and found barrels of distilled water in the back of the storeroom. By the time he'd rolled one of them into the bathroom, Kareena was naked. She ran over and kissed him. With considerable self-control, Blade managed not to put his arms around her. He thought she looked disappointed. Then she frowned.

"Blade, do you suppose there are any ghosts here?"

Blade felt a moment's irritation at this superstition, then remembered his own feeling when he had stared at Mossev's dead towers in the evening light. He shook his head. "I

don't think any of the Tower Builders died here. Even if
they did, in England we think that to bring life back to a
place where there are ghosts drives away the evil ones and
gives peace to the good ones." Cautiously he reached out
and laid a hand on the smooth skin of her left shoulder.
She did not flinch, and her eyes continued to meet his.
"We're alive, aren't we?"

"Yes," said Kareena. She raised a hand and covered his.
"We're alive." She lifted his hand, held it for a moment,
then moved it down onto her right breast. She squeezed
her eyes shut, and they stood like that for a moment. Then
she raised a hand and began caressing Blade's neck and
throat.

"Kareena," he said. "Do you know what you're doing?"
He thought he had his answer in the way her nipple was
turning hard under his hand, but he wanted to be certain.

She took another step closer to him. "Yes, Blade. I
know. Now both hands went to work, unbuttoning Blade's
jacket. He shrugged himself free of it, then ran his hands
up and down Kareena's back. He knelt as she struggled to
pull the shirt over his head. When she'd succeeded, he
gripped her neat, solid buttocks firmly and began kissing
her smooth stomach. He ran his lips up over her ribcage
and she sighed louder. So did Blade. He'd never expected
to find a woman's ribcage a beautiful sight, but there was a
first time for everything. When Blade's lips encircled a
nipple, Kareena gave a little choking cry. When he ran one
hand lightly up between her thighs to the damp hair where
they joined, he could feel her trembling so hard he was
afraid she would fall.

"Blade." His name came out barely recognizable.
"Blade. The beds."

He stood up and kissed her lips, pulling her close until
he could feel her swollen nipples and she groaned at the
feeling of his erection against her thighs. Her mouth flared
open and her tongue leaped out to seek him.

"Kareena. . . ."

They managed to get out of the bathroom, but they
never got to the bedrooms. Their desire was too strong and
one of the reclining couches was too close at hand. Kareena
bent down and swiftly unfastened Blade's trousers. It took

her a little longer to find the catch on the silver loinguard. Then she would have kissed his erection if he hadn't pulled her away just in time. Blade knew that Kareena's lips on top of everything else would cause him to have a climax then and there. If she was a virgin he was going to have enough trouble controlling himself to give her what she desperately wanted and certainly deserved.

Blade was right about Kareena's being a virgin, but he'd underestimated how eager she was. She practically pushed him down onto the couch, without even giving him time to finish taking off his trousers. She needed no guiding to straddle him, and he needed no guiding to slide smoothly into her warm, damp readiness. The moment of resistance came and went so swiftly that Blade could hardly be sure it happened at all, and Kareena's eyes were already squeezed tightly shut. Her mouth opened, and it gaped wider as she threw her head back. Her body swayed like a tree in a high wind.

Blade hoped he could last. Then Kareena started squirming from side to side as her own control slipped, and Blade knew that his was going to vanish entirely in another moment. So he gripped her by the shoulders and pulled her hard toward him, until his lips could work all over her breasts. She bent over even farther and bit him in the neck so hard he yelled, and thoughts of vampires ran weirdly through his mind.

Then she cried out, too, even louder. Blade felt her writhing and twisting inside as well as outside for one fleeting moment. Then he felt nothing except his own explosive release, as he drained himself into Kareena.

For a short time the ceiling could have fallen in without either of the people sprawled on the couch noticing it. Then Kareena slowly curled herself onto Blade's sweat-speckled chest. He noticed she was very careful to keep him inside her, and he was happy to stay there.

"You said we would do nothing which was not for the good of Kaldak," he murmured in her ear. "Was this for the good of Kaldak?"

"I don't know what it did for Kaldak," said Kareena. "But it was certainly good for me."

Chapter 13

After a while Blade and Kareena felt like moving again. They took a bath, using up most of the spray soap and making a happy mess on the floor. At the finish Kareena was kneeling in front of Blade, sponging off his thighs and groin. At last she threw the sponge away, ran her hands up between Blade's thighs, and followed with her mouth. They quickly wound up on the couch for a second time. Kareena seemed willing to make up for what she lacked in experience, with her enthusiasm and willingness to try anything.

Both of them would have enjoyed a third time, but Blade couldn't forget the long shaft leading to the surface. He was sure the Doimari knew of the defeat of their waldo, and would react to it sooner or later. He didn't want to find them waiting at the mouth of the tunnel, a dozen laser rifles or another waldo ready to fry anyone who came out.

He kissed Kareena, then swung his legs off the couch, and patted her gently on the rump. "It's time we were on our way out of here," he said. "If we stay much longer, we'll be sacrificing the good of Kaldak to our own pleasure." He walked over to the packs and started rummaging through them. "Now if I can just find something to use for a booby trap—"

Kareena sat up. "A what?"

"A booby trap." Although he knew that every minute might count, Blade took the time to explain what he meant. He might be killed, and if he wasn't he would sooner or later be returning to Home Dimension. The more of his knowledge of the fine points of handling Oltec he

89

passed along to Kareena, the better for Kaldak and the Land.

"Watch what I do very carefully," he finished. "That way you can teach the Kaldakans to do it, if I am not around. You can also warn the Kaldakans who come to this place, so they will not fall into the traps I set for the Doimari. If I can set any traps, that is," he added. So far he hadn't found anything he could use in the packs. They couldn't afford the time for another complete search of the whole complex, but he hated leaving this wealth of Oltec for the Doimari.

Toward the bottom of Kareena's pack Blade found a ridged metal ball with a ring on top. It looked remarkably like an old-fashioned hand grenade. It exploded like one, too, when Blade tested it by pulling the pin and dropping it down the shaft. The Tower Builders hadn't abandoned reliable older weapons while developing new ones. Blade pointed this out as an example of their wisdom.

"So we should not give up bows even when rifles are as common as bows are now?" asked Kareena.

"No. The bows will still be good for hunting. Every animal you kill with an arrow saves power cells for killing Doimari."

Kareena remembered where she'd found the grenade and led Blade to the room. He picked up all the grenades he could carry. Then he booby trapped the entrance to the shaft with four grenades wired to the door. Any unsuspecting visitor opening the door would stretch an almost invisible wire, pulling the pin out of one grenade and setting off the rest. Then Blade and Kareena slung their packs and started climbing.

Halfway up the shaft Blade burned off ten rungs of the ladder, leaving a fifteen-foot gap. At intervals from there to the top he cut halfway through a rung. Each rung still looked sound, but under a man's weight it would break and drop an incautious climber several hundred feet to the bottom of the shaft. Kareena watched carefully, asking questions whenever she didn't understand what Blade was doing. Sometimes he laughed grimly at the thought of the fate awaiting unsuspecting Doimari.

They saw no sign of any unwanted visitors in the storeroom. Blade and Kareena left some of the items they'd collected below, then filled up the space in their packs with power cells. As far as Blade was concerned, they couldn't have too much power for their rifles. Then they started up the tunnel. Halfway up, Blade used all but two of the remaining hand grenades to set another booby trap.

"Won't that bring down the whole tunnel?" asked Kareena.

"I hope it will," said Blade. "It's better that no one have the Oltec here than that the Doimari use it in the war."

Kareena looked stunned for a moment, then nodded slowly. "Yes, I suppose it is so. With ten thousand men armed with that Oltec, the Doimari would not even need the war machines."

Blade would have liked to kiss her for such clear thinking, but the tunnel was too narrow. Instead he simply squeezed her hand, then started climbing again. As they approached the mouth of the tunnel, Blade found himself stopping every few yards and holding his breath. He heard nothing except his own heartbeat and a faint distant sighing which might have been the wind in the street.

They'd stayed underground longer than he thought. When they finally crawled out of the tunnel, it was so dark outside that Blade could barely find the hole in the wall made by the waldo. "Oh, good," whispered Kareena. "It will be easier to escape in the darkness."

"Perhaps," said Blade. "But there is Oltec which lets a man see in the dark almost as well as in the light." He explained infrared searchlights and gunsights in language he hoped Kareena could understand. Relying on his own excellent night vision, Blade studied the room. He saw no signs anyone had entered it since the Kaldakans left. There didn't seem to be anything to be gained by waiting longer.

"Come on, Kareena."

They'd taken no more than a dozen steps beyond the door when the trap closed. Two laser beams blazed down from a window across the street, striking just above the hole made by the waldo. A dry patch of climbing vine caught fire. The flames were almost as good as a flare for lighting up the street. Kareena screamed, started to run back toward the building, then pulled herself to a stop.

"Come on! They've got that way covered!" Blade shouted. Then another laser fired from their left, the beam going so wide that it was either a bad shot or a deliberate miss. Blade didn't care. Charging at even a bad marksman armed with a laser was simply committing suicide. He jerked Kareena around to the right, then pushed her toward the far side of the street. If she got close enough to the buildings, the snipers in the window couldn't see her.

Blade raised his own rifle, waited until the next shot from the left, and saw it go even wider than the first one. This was puzzling but it also gave him a target. A quick shot from Blade brought a scream and the clatter of a falling weapon. The remaining snipers in the window fired again, but now they seemed unsure whether they should aim at Blade or at Kareena. They missed both, then Kareena was close under the window. Blade came up behind her, pulled the pin out of a grenade, and got ready to heave it up into the window. If the Doimari were relying too much on their weapons and were too thin on the ground to meet a determined effort to break out—

Something went *whump* in the darkness behind Blade, and something else went *wsssshhhhhh* in the darkness overhead. "Get down!" he yelled, and dove for the ground as the pavement around them erupted in flame and flying debris. Kareena was still on her feet when the blast caught her and dashed her to the ground like a doll. A second explosion went off, then a third and a fourth beside the building over the tunnel. Five, six, seven—Blade lost count and hugged the pavement, hands over his ears, not sure that his last moments hadn't come and only hoping the Doimari would wipe out half their own men with all the explosives they were throwing.

Dust was still settling around Blade when he saw dark-clad men converge on Kareena. She tried to get to her feet, one leg buckled under her, and she fell again with a throat-tearing scream of agony. She still had her sword and the courage to use it. A man who moved in too close screamed even louder than Kareena when her sword's point went into his groin. Then one man stamped down on Kareena's sword hand, another kicked her in the stomach, and several more fell on her.

As they did, Blade rose to his feet. He was an ice-cold killing machine now, mind and body united to serve only one goal: killing as many Doimari was possible before he went down himself. Firing from the hip, he swept the beam of his rifle back and forth. Doimari howled and fell on top of Kareena. Blade shut his ears against the cries, waiting for a return laser blast in his guts or a grenade explosion tearing him apart, vaguely surprised when neither happened.

Too late he heard footsteps behind him. He was turning, rifle still firing, when the net fell over his head and shoulders. He held onto the rifle with one hand and tried to lift the net clear with the other. A sudden jerk on the net pulled him over backward. He struck his head so hard that for a moment comets and fireworks blazed in the darkness. He felt utterly disgusted with himself at falling into a trap so quickly that he couldn't even give Kareena a clean death.

Then clubs smashed down at every exposed part of his body, and Richard Blade no longer felt anything at all.

"My name is Nungor," said a wavering, distorted voice in the distance. Blade could barely make out the words over the roaring and hissing in his ears. "Are you the man called Blade of England?" More roaring and hissing. "Are you?" Then silence, and suddenly a deluge of cold water descending from nowhere onto Blade's head. The roaring and hissing faded away, although they left behind aches and pains in a good many parts of Blade's body. He also discovered that his hands were bound behind his back with wire. Then he found himself staring up at a brown face with a dirty black beard and a dirty green patch over one eye.

"I am Nungor," the face said again. "Are you Blade of England?"

"Since you already know my name—" began Blade, then gritted his teeth as someone clubbed him across the shin. Nungor spun around and yelled at a man Blade couldn't see.

"No, you rat's bastard! The woman, the woman only! Feragga wants this one!" Then Nungor bent over and jerked Blade up into a sitting position. Blade saw that the man was no more than five feet four inches tall, but nearly as wide, and all of it was solid muscle with scars on every inch of exposed skin.

"You *are* Blade of England, aren't you?" said Nungor, an edge in his voice. Then he shook his head. "It won't be you paying the price for not talking. It will be Peython's daughter." He pointed. Blade saw Kareena spread-eagled on the ground, wrists and ankles tied to heavy stones with wire. Blood oozed from around the wires. She looked as if she'd been run over by a truck, with face and thighs horribly bruised, a dozen cuts crusted over with dried blood, and a crude bandage on her left leg. Half a dozen men were standing around her, holding a variety of weapons and tools.

Nungor took Blade's hesitation for resistance and signaled to one of his men. A spear butt thumped down hard on Kareena's bandaged leg. Unfortunately she was conscious. Blade saw her arch her body and bite her already blood-caked lips. The spear butt came down again, and she gasped. It was coming down a third time when Blade said sharply, "I am Blade of England. What else do you want to know?"

He hoped he hadn't given in too easily, but he would rather let Nungor think he was weak than let Kareena be tortured anymore. It looked as if she'd already been through the mill to the point where she couldn't take much more punishment. As long as there was any hope, Blade intended to get both himself and Kareena out of the hands of the Doimari. That meant doing whatever might be needed to keep her alive.

Nungor jerked his head at the men around Kareena, and the spear butt thumped harmlessly on the ground. "Very wise, Blade. Very wise. We may yet be able to talk."

"That is not yet certain, Nungor. You know you have Peython's daughter. Don't you also know that she's worth more as a live hostage than as a mangled corpse?" Normally Blade would have tried to deny that this was Kareena, but if Nungor knew who he was he would doubtless know who she was as well. Doimar's spies had done better work in Kaldak than Peython would be happy to hear.

94

"I know she is worth more alive than dead. But compared to you she is worth nothing at all. You have knowledge not only from Kaldak but from your land of England. Do not waste my time with arguing, either." He signaled to his men and they formed a circle around Kareena, hiding her. What happened inside that circle Blade never knew, but he never forgot Kareena's scream either.

Whatever else happens, I am not going to leave this Dimension without killing Nungor, even if it means my own death. That resolution calmed Blade, so that he was able to tell Nungor enough to save Kareena from further torture without revealing too much about the Kaldakan expedition. He would have liked to be able to lie about the discovery of the complex at the bottom of the shaft but decided not to risk putting Kareena in danger. There was also the matter of the booby traps he'd left below, which Blade had no intention of revealing. Nungor seemed to have no more than twenty men with him. If half of them went down from the booby traps and didn't come back up, it might be worth trying to wipe out the rest and escape.

"Did Bairam leave any traps in the tunnel?" asked Nungor at last.

Blade frowned, trying to look uncertain. "I heard some of his men speaking of doing this. I do not know if there are any, or where there are. They would not trust me with the knowledge."

"That is more wisdom than I would expect of Bairam," said Nungor. "Blade, I think you are lying." He raised a hand to the men around Kareena. Before they could move, Blade was on his feet. Nungor jumped back and drew his sword, obviously impressed at Blade's size and his feat of jumping up with his hands still tied behind his back.

"Nungor, hear me," said Blade. "You can chop Kareena into small pieces if you wish. I cannot stop you. I can keep you from gaining anything by it, however.

"I know the fighting arts of England. I can make you choose between killing me or dying yourself. When I am dead, all my knowledge of Kaldak and England will be dead with me. Even if I do not kill you, I wonder if you will live long after your mistress Feragga hears our tale. You will have done a foolish thing. I have not heard that

Feragga of Doimar is gentle with fools, or keeps them long in her service."

That was only a guess, based on what Blade had heard of the ruling lady of Doimar. Apparently it was a good one. Nungor took another step backward, and Blade thought he saw the man swallow. Then the Doimari shrugged.

"Very well, Blade. It seems that you know how to put yourself in a strong position even when a prisoner."

"I have traveled in many lands, Nungor. If I had feared death, it would long since have taken me. As a warrior, I am sure you know this as well as I do."

Nungor jerked his head, acknowledging the praise. Then he pointed to one of the men around Kareena. "Yabo. Take three men and go down. Take bags and bring up as many fire boxes as you can carry."

"Yes, *Shro* Nungor."

Blade mentally erased the idea of trying to escape while Yabo and his squad were down the tunnel. Four down left sixteen on the surface—too many, unless matters got so desperate that it was simply a question of finding a clean death.

Yabo and his men marched off briskly and disappeared into the basement. Blade sat down and leaned back against the nearest wall, working his concealed hands back and forth steadily. The wire was tight, but it felt brittle enough to break if he worked at it long enough. Maybe the Doimari wouldn't spring the trap in the tunnel. In that case by the time they got to the one in the shaft, they'd have more men down below and Kareena would have recovered a little strength. It wasn't completely impossible that—

Whrrrrummmmmppppp!

A cloud of dust, smoke, and fragments shot out of the basement like the blast from a cannon. One of the booby traps had been sprung! Nungor's men jumped up with shouts and curses. One had his mouth open when a flying fragment hit him in the stomach and smashed him against the wall. Then a second explosion came, with a long hissing sound. A wavering blue light shone in the heart of the smoke cloud. Some of the power cells had been affected by

96

the grenade explosions and were burning themselves out. Blade tried to take shallow breaths as the smoke and fumes filled the street. All around him, half-invisible in the murk, he heard Nungor's men coughing and choking. Then above that sound he heard a long drawn-out rumble, growing steadily until it seemed as if the earth itself would start shaking any minute.

Blade knew it was no earthquake. Through gaps in the murk he saw the walls of the building swaying and cracking, then shedding pieces themselves the size of a small house. Shaken by the waldo's attack, the explosions last night, the booby trap, and finally the power cells, the building was collapsing.

Then the roar increased until Blade had to open his mouth to equalize the pressure on his ears. The dust billowed so thickly that he could barely see Nungor's men around Kareena. Then he saw them break and run, as fear of the unknown overcame their fear of Nungor. Nungor vanished on their heels, shouting curses and waving his sword, and Blade was alone with Kareena.

He made one last furious effort against the wire on his wrists, felt metal gouge skin and flesh, then felt the wires snap. His hands were free.

Blade reached Kareena in three long steps and bent down to shout in her ear. "Kareena! Can you hear me?" He thought he saw her nod, even though her eyes were closed. "I'm going to cut you loose, and we'll try—"

Kareena's eyes opened, and she licked dust-caked lips. "Blade, you've got to run! I can't come with you. My leg—it's broken. Don't—"

Blade swore under his breath. He should have thought of this possibility, but he'd been too concerned with keeping the girl from being tortured to death. "Then I'll stay with you."

"Blade, you can't—"

"Kareena, I will. Now close your eyes and pretend to be unconscious again." He wanted to add, "And say your prayers," because he wasn't at all sure what mood Nungor would be in when he returned.

Slowly the crash and roar of the falling building died

away. The breeze thinned the fog of dust until Blade could see nearly fifty feet. At the limit of his vision was Nungor, holding a laser rifle aimed at Blade.

Blade slowly stood up, shifting his footing as he did so that he was in position to strike down at Kareena's ribs with one heel. That would give her a merciful death, before Nungor could kill him with the rifle. Nungor could either kill them both or spare them both. Blade refused to consider giving the man any other choices.

His unspoken message seemed to reach the Doimari leader. Slowly Nungor lowered his rifle. "It seems your honor binds you to Peython's daughter, England-man."

"It seems so."

"Well, then I shall do nothing to you for now. Whether Feragga will be so gentle, I do not know."

"That is for Feragga to say."

"True."

Blade looked at Kareena and winked. He thought he saw her wink back. Then he turned to look at what was left of the building. A short stretch of wall about three stories high was the only thing still standing from a building eight stories high and a block square. It would take a Home Dimension engineering crew months to dig anything out from under that hill of rubble. In this Dimension it would take years. Whoever won the war might someday dig out the treasure below, but it would play no part in the war itself.

That wasn't a bad day's work, for two nearly helpless captives. Blade sat down and watched Nungor's men trickling back, under the lash of their chief's curses. None of them came anywhere near either of the prisoners.

Chapter 14

The Doimari left Gilmarg before noon that day. Blade walked, his hands unbound but several rifle-armed guards always close at hand. Kareena was loaded onto the back of a munfan like a sack of loot. She was obviously in pain, but Blade noted that her broken leg had been thoroughly splinted. He knew she would have an uncomfortable trip, but it should not be a fatal one unless the broken leg became infected.

The expedition set such a pace that the towers of Doimar were in sight by noon on the fifth day. By then Kareena's bruises were healing, and her broken leg showed no sign of infection. It still gave her so much pain that Blade knew the escape from Doimar would have to wait until Kareena could walk or until he found some sort of vehicle.

Both choices had their dangers. The first would mean staying in Doimar at the mercy of a notoriously merciless ruler for weeks or even months. Apart from the danger to Blade and Kareena, there was the danger that Feragga would launch her armies and waldoes against Kaldak before the prisoners could escape with their knowledge. The second course could get them home more quickly, but this was far from certain. There might not be any vehicles. Even if there were, finding one could take as much time as the healing of Kareena's leg. It would certainly take a good deal of luck, or else the cooperation of the Doimari themselves in giving Blade freedom to explore their city.

Blade decided he'd have to try winning over the Doimari, and he could see only one way of doing this. He would have to pretend to change sides as soon as he could do so convincingly. After that, he would have a better chance of learning anything he wanted to know, including Feragga's war plans as well as how to escape.

There would still be dangers and disadvantages. The Doimari might learn too much about Kaldak from him while he was learning about them. He hoped to avoid that by mostly telling lies about England's Oltec. Thinking the man she loved was a traitor to Kaldak would make Kareena's captivity still more unpleasant, and there was nothing at all Blade could do about that. He had to be completely convincing, and he was afraid he could not be if anyone but himself knew that he was acting.

Finally, there was always the possibility that when the time came there would still be no way for both him and Kareena to escape. Then Blade would have to face an ugly choice. He could stay in Doimar and really betray Kaldak, or escape himself, perhaps save Kaldak, but condemn Kareena to a thoroughly unpleasant death. He knew she would ask him to leave if she knew the truth, but he still didn't like to think of facing Peython and Bairam after leaving her to die.

At least he wouldn't have to think about this any more for a few weeks.

Feragga of Doimar looked enough like her *Shro* (War Captain) Nungor to be his older sister, although she could easily have picked him up under one arm. She was inches taller and wider across the shoulder than Blade and probably weighed more. She still moved with an ease and grace which hinted that very little of her bulk was fat. Her round face with its oversized nose could hardly be called attractive, but she looked shrewd and tough, a leader who'd be no easier to fool than Peython. Blade could only hope that her eagerness for knowledge useful in her war would make her ready to meet his demands.

He stood before Feragga in the smoke-darkened chamber which served as her combination throne room and banquet hall, listening to Nungor tell of the battle in Gilmarg. Blade was still unbound and still closely guarded. Kareena sat tied to a portable aluminum chair. The room was bare

100

of decoration, and practically everyone in sight was either an armed fighter or a scantily-clad slave.

"Well, Blade of England," said Feragga. "You are not of Kaldak, so my war against them is not against you unless you wish it so. You can be a guest in Doimar, or you can be a prisoner. If you wish to be a prisoner, I have nothing more to say to you. It will then be those whose business it is to learn secrets who will be dealing with you and Kareena. When they are through, what is left of you will be given to our Seekers for Health to study."

Blade nodded. This was about what he'd expected. He still didn't want to appear to be giving in at the first threat. "You speak plainly, Feragga of Doimar. In England we value that. So I will speak plainly in return. What am I offered if I would rather be a guest?" He tried to shut his ears against Kareena's gasp.

"That is hard to say, Blade" replied Feragga. "It depends on what you do for Doimar. If you teach us all that is known in England . . . ." She shrugged, implying that in such a case the sky was the limit.

Blade shook his head. "I cannot teach all that is known in England. I'm a warrior, not one of England's Seekers."

"You seem to know as much as any Seeker in War or Seeker of Machines," said Nungor. This seemed to confirm Blade's guess that the Seekers were Doimar's "scientists." The city must have scientists to be able to go so far beyond the other cities of the Land in recovering the knowledge of Oltec. Again he shook his head.

"I have traveled in many lands besides England. A warrior must keep his eyes and ears open as he travels. Otherwise he does not live to travel far. While watching for enemies, one can also see many strange machines and new ways of war."

"That is the truth," said Feragga. "It is a truth which some in Doimar who think themselves wise do not yet admit." She glowered around the room without looking at anyone in particular. "So you do not know all that is known in England. You still know much which is not known in the Land. Will you teach it all to us in Doimar?"

"Yes," said Blade, smiling. "I have seen Kaldak, and now I have seen Doimar. I know which of the two cities is

101

more fit to rule the Land." He bowed elaborately to Feragga.

Kareen made a strangled noise, then shouted, "Blade, you dirty—!" That was as far as she got before Nungor stepped up to her chair and slapped her twice. She spat in his face. He grabbed her hair with one hand and drew the other fist back for a blow which would certainly have knocked out most of her teeth.

"Hold, Nungor!" Feragga shouted. Her insolence will be punished enough. Clearly she will be no proper slave, until she is initiated. But if you beat her now, she will not feel the Initiation as she should."

Nungor reluctantly let go of Kareena. "That is true, Feragga." Blade could have sworn he licked his lips, and several of the people around the room wore looks of obscene anticipation. Blade suddenly knew that he had to try to protect Kareena from the Initiation, even at some risk to his cover story. It sounded like an ordeal which she might not survive in her weakened condition.

"Feragga, I ask as my first gift Kareena, daughter of Peython, as my slave. If this is granted, I will initiate her myself, according to the Law of England."

Nungor's eyes narrowed. "I thought you and she were sworn freemates?"

"Indeed I told you so," said Blade. He kept his eyes fixed on Feragga. He doubted that if he looked toward Kareena he could get this lie out with a straight face. "That does not mean I told the truth."

"No doubt. But if you lied to me then, why should you not be lying to Ferraga now?" said Nungor.

The little War Captain was much too shrewd for Blade's peace of mind. Blade smiled blandly. "I know the reputation of Feragga of Doimar too well to lie to her. Do you think me a fool, Nungor? Also, when I met you I had not seen Doimar itself. I could not judge which side I was on. Now I have seen your city and know better."

There was a long silence, in which Blade measured the distance between him and the nearest guard armed with a laser rifle. It was just short enough. If this attempt to save Kareena from torture failed, he was sure he could grab the rifle before anyone could stop him, then Feragga, Nungor, and Kareena would all die before he went down himself.

Feragga broke the silence with a harsh laugh. "Well, Blade, I see you are not going to be an easy man to buy, or a cheap one. Never mind. If you are worth your price, I shall not grudge it. When the time comes, Kareena shall be the first part of your price. A pity we can't get some work out of her in the meantime, but that is as it must be. Take her out."

Four slaves carried Kareena's chair out of the room. As the door closed behind her, a weight seemed to lift from Blade's shoulders. Knowing that Kareena would not be hearing any more of what he said would make the rest of this meeting far easier.

Feragga promised Blade a sword, living quarters, and food, women if he wanted them, and whatever knowledge of Doimar's Oltec he might need. In return he would teach the Doimari all he had learned on his travels or in England, particularly anything which might aid the Doimari in their war for the rulership of the Land.

When that war was won, the rewards would be great. Kareena would be only the first of them. Blade would have land and loot from Kaldak or any other city he chose, rank and power in the new Doimari Empire, and a place close to Feragga herself. *How close*? Blade wondered. From the look in the woman's eyes he suspected she might want him as a bedmate. From the look in Nungor's eyes, the War Captain suspected the same thing and didn't like the idea at all.

Blade left, fairly certain that Nungor was going to be his real enemy. Feragga was sufficiently eager for Blade's knowledge and perhaps his body to give him the benefit of the doubt. Nungor was suspicious and would have plenty of chances to confirm those suspicions.

Blade wasn't seriously worried. He'd faced and beaten more formidable opponents than Nungor. At the same time, he felt that the gift he would like most in all the world or any Dimension was not having to tell anyone a single lie for a whole month!

In Feragga's own tower at least, the Doimari had the elevators working again. Blade was given a suite of three rooms on a high floor, with a guard at the door but no bars on the window. They weren't needed. Outside the window was a three-hundred-foot drop straight down to the courtyard of the tower.

Blade saw there was more metal in the furniture than he'd seen in Peython's tower. Otherwise there was hardly anything in his rooms which could teach him much about Doimar. He tested the lock on the outer door, discovered that it worked, and set it. Then he walked back to the window and looked down into the courtyard.

It was late afternoon, and the towers of Doimar were stretching long shadows across the lower buildings. The towers to the west were silhouetted against a reddening sky. In the courtyard a company of soldiers was drilling. Blade counted about two hundred men. They were going through the sort of close-order drill loved by sergeants in every Dimension, whether it makes any sense on the battlefield or not.

Blade also noted that every one of the men had a laser rifle and that many seemed to be carrying grenades. At one end of the courtyard a small group of men was standing around what looked like mortars or light artillery. There were no waldoes in sight, but Blade hadn't expected that any of Doimar's secret weapons would be on public display. Peython must have taken as much trouble to send spies into Doimar as Feragga had to send them into Kaldak, although he hadn't learned as much.

Blade thought of Kaldak, with at most one laser rifle for every four men or women of fighting age and no other Oltec weapons at all. It didn't really matter that Doimar's soldiers were wasting their time in close-order drill. Even without the robots, the weapons they already carried would give them an enormous advantage in firepower. They could probably win if they were trained to walk backward on their hands and fire their rifles with their toes! The idea of an army marching into battle like that made Blade laugh, but there was nothing funny about what would happen to Kaldak and the other cities of the Land when Feragga's army advanced.

To be sure, she would destroy the iron grip of the Law and its restrictions on the use of Oltec. She would also be destroying many lives and much wealth, and reducing to slavery the surviving inhabitants of any city she conquered. Doimar could only end up ruling an empire of ruins, inhabited by slaves or by outlaws determined to die rather than yield to their conquerors. In the process most of the civilization built up since the fall of the Sky Masters would be destroyed. The Land would sink back into barbarism, and this time the darkness would last not for hundreds but for thousands of years.

On the other hand, the defeat of Doimar would not mean the victory of the Law and its fear of Oltec. Kaldak was already well started on the road to exploring beyond the Law and making positive improvements in the Land. But it would have to go even farther in order to beat Doimar. Where one city went, others would sooner or later have to follow, out of fear or simply out of pride.

Blade knew where he stood. Doimar had to be stopped. The only question was *how*, and there was no point in even asking himself that until he knew more.

Sharp knocking on the door interrupted Blade's thoughts. He took his sword from the windowsill and faced the door. "Who is there, and what do you want?"

"Nungor, Blade. I have brought a woman for you."

"I—" Blade was about to say, "I did not ask for a woman," then stopped himself. If Nungor was bringing him a woman, it was probably to make Feragga jealous. Making relations between Feragga and her War Captain as bad as possible could do more good than harm, as long as it didn't put Kareena in more danger.

Also, this would be Blade's first chance to talk to a Doimari slave. From experience in many Dimensions he knew that slaves could be good sources of information on their masters' strengths and weaknesses. It was not only what they said, it was also what they didn't say.

"Send her in, Nungor. I thank you."

There were two girls, neither more than seventeen, both dressed only in dirty gray shifts. One was thin, almost gaunt, while the other was positively plump. There was also a boy who couldn't have been more than fifteen, wearing only a loincloth and clearly frightened half out of his wits. The moment Nungor closed the door, the boy scurried

105

across the room to the corner farthest from Blade and cowered there, baring his teeth like a cornered rat.

Blade tried to soothe him. "Do not worry. I am not a lover of men. Even if I was, you are too young for me, by the Law of England."

"England is a city with—?" began the slim girl. The other one struck her sharply across the mouth.

"You talk only when the man says you can, little fool! Didn't your Initiation teach you anything?"

The slim girl knelt at Blade's feet, eyes on the floor. "You may beat me before you take your pleasure with me, Master."

"No doubt I may," said Blade dryly. "But I do not choose to. I will always forgive *one* mistake." He pulled off his shirt. "Now—into the bed with you." He felt no real desire for these two poor creatures, but if he didn't take them Nungor might get suspicious, and the girls would surely be punished. He could hardly let them suffer for his scruples. The slim girl pulled her shift over her head and started toward the bed. As she did, Blade saw her back.

"Good God!"

She stopped as if he'd struck her, quivering all over. He stared at her. In spite of her thinness, she was quite lovely, with the taut, spare curves of a girl who's just turned into a woman—except for her back. From just below her shoulder blades to the base of her spine, her back was a ridged mess of criss-crossing scars. She must have been flogged half to death and would certainly carry scars like that to the end of her life.

"That was your Initiation—the flogging?" asked Blade gently. In spite of his tone the girl seemed too frightened to speak, so her companion spoke for her.

"Yes. She and the boy there were made slaves when their parents refused to pay their taxes. She was unruly and disobedient, so she was Initiated by the whip. The boy was even worse, so he was Initiated with the knife."

Blade decided not to ask what "Initiation with the knife" meant. He didn't really need to know. He did know that he would have to be more careful than ever, if "Initiation" for Kareena meant being flogged like this. He doubted if either her mind or her body could survive the experience.

106

"You have not been Initiated?" he asked the second girl.

"I?" She looked insulted. "Only a fool sells herself into slavery, then says what she should not. I found an easier life in Feragga's house than I could ever have outside." She pulled her shift over her head and raised her arms over her head. "Have I not done well?"

She certainly looked well-fed, almost complacent, although the other girl would have been much more attractive without the scars and her fear. Blade sat down on the windowsill, pulled off his boots, and began undoing his trousers.

As his silver loinguard came into sight, both girls stared. The scarred girl was the bolder of the two. She reached out a finger and touched the metal, then jerked her hand back as if the loinguard was red-hot.

"You may speak," Blade said. They were both obviously dying of curiosity.

"Is—do you have—your power in *that*?" said the plump girl. "Do you—keep it on?"

Blade laughed. "No. My power is where it is in any other man." He unhooked the loinguard, took it off, and held it up in front of the girls so they could see it more clearly. "You see. It is only a thing of Oltec, to protect me in battle, so that I will not lose the place where my power stays."

"Ah," they said almost in unison. Then also in unison they reached out and started stroking Blade's thighs and penis. This led to the inevitable conclusion, although Blade could never use the term "making love" when he spoke of what he did in the bed with the two slave girls. He'd had much more pleasant erotic experiences with women he'd seduced as part of an assignment. At least the two girls seemed happy enough, probably at knowing they would not be punished for failing to please him.

When he'd finished with the girls, Blade walked over to the boy still cowering in the corner. "If you wish either of the girls, and she consents, I will let you have her. I will even go into one of the other rooms and leave you alone."

The boy stared at Blade as if he'd grown a second head, then burst into tears and curled up almost in the fetal position. In the process his loincloth slipped. Blade had a strong

107

stomach, and he'd seen more ghastly sights than any other six men he knew put together. He still had to swallow and close his eyes for a moment at the sight of the boy's groin. It was nothing but a mass of scar tissue. He'd been castrated, so crudely and brutally that it was a miracle he was still alive.

Blade sighed. There was nothing to say to the boy and nothing to say even to himself except what he'd already said a number of times: Doimar had to be stopped.

He helped the boy to his feet, then called the guards. The two girls were supporting the boy between them as the guards led all three of them out. Blade stood with his face firmly turned to the window until he heard the door close behind him. He did not want anyone who might inform Feragga or Nungor to see the look on his face.

The sun was close to the horizon now. Most of Doimar's towers still had part of their metal facing, and these reflected the reddish sunset over the rest of the city. It looked almost as if the entire city had been dipped in blood. Blade thought this was a highly appropriate color for Doimar.

Chapter 15

Blade soon learned there were two factions in Doimar's army. One was led by the Seekers. These rule-of-thumb scientists and engineers had rediscovered most of the military Oltec. Their faction included the men and women trained to operate the waldoes, and certain others with rare technical skills.

The second faction was led by the older officers, who'd learned warfare before Feragga became ruler of Doimar.

They had the support of the infantry, who would fight with nothing but rifles, grenades, and some mortars.

The infantry faction should have won by sheer weight of numbers. Doimar's infantry counted at least seven thousand men and women, while the Seekers could call on the support of no more than five or six hundred. However, even the infantrymen usually admitted that the waldoes would be nearly indispensable in the war against the other cities of the Land. They resented this fact, but they didn't deny it. By the time Blade reached Doimar, the two factions had signed an uneasy truce. This didn't keep either one from seeking to gain whatever advantage it could over the other, by fair means or foul.

It helped keep the peace that Feragga and Nungor both tried to be impartial, at least in public. Both learned swordsmanship, became experts with rifles, and could handle grenades and mortars. Both also knew how to operate the waldoes and put them through their paces. But it was still no secret that Feragga's sympathies lay with the Seekers, and Nungor's lay with the infantry.

None of this surprised Blade at all. In any army, those who do their fighting with machinery seldom get along with those who expose their own bodies to the enemy's weapons. The machine operators think the infantrymen are stupid. The infantrymen think the machine operators are cowards. In Doimar matters were even worse than usual. Blade had learned that the waldoes were operated by some sort of remote control, and thus the waldo operators would be many miles from the battlefield, doing their work with all the comforts of home around them. The infantry would be out in front, hungry, cold, thirsty, stinking, and dying in the mud like the infantry of every army in every Dimension throughout history. Blade was quite sure that each side in the feud would try to win him over. When this happened, he was almost as sure he could get some advantage from it.

The training room was two hundred feet long and a hundred feet wide, with an arched roof eighty feet high. At the far end one of the waldoes stood to the right of a tall steel door. At the near end stood Blade, a female Seeker, one of the control chairs for the waldoes, and several electronic consoles. The chair and the consoles stood on a rubber-tired cart.

Blade contemplated the control chair. It reminded him of the equipment once used to send him into Dimension X, before the invention of the KALI capsule. There was the same chair with a polished steel frame and black leather seat and back. There was the same tangle of multicolored wires crawling all over it like demented snakes. It looked like something you'd expect to find in the dungeons of the Spanish Inquisition.

There were also a few differences. The chair and its wiring stood in the middle of a steel frame eight feet high. From the frame hung long metallic mesh gloves and a helmet which covered the whole head and bulged with electronic and optical gear. Knee-high mesh boots stood on the base of the frame.

"Now listen carefully, Blade of England," said the Seeker sharply. "To work the Fighting Machines is not as simple as it looks. Many have thought so. Their mistakes have damaged many machines. We do not often let fighters of Doimar near a Voice Chair until we have tested them in many ways. But it is Feragga's order that you are to be taught everything you want to learn. We obey her orders." She shook her fist in his face. "But if you wreck a Machine, nothing Feragga says will save you from me."

The Seeker had to reach up to shake her fist in Blade's face. She was hardly more than five feet tall, with a trim figure showing through a sort of uniform of green leather trousers and shirt. Her dark eyes were enormous.

"I will listen and not wreck a Machine," said Blade. "In England the best warriors are trained to use both the weapons of their bodies and the weapons of Oltec. Only those who know both can command in war."

"If that is truly the case in England, you are wiser than we," said the woman. "As it is, we who know the Machines must often give way to those who know nothing but a child's weapons. If Feragga was not wise, we would be as badly off as the people of Kaldak, chained by the Law."

She started explaining the operation of the waldoes. It was very much as Blade had expected, a masterpiece of simplicity. The waldo operator put his hands into the gloves and his feet into the boots. Then every motion of his arms and legs was transmitted by radio to the waldo, which matched those movements. The helmet contained video and sound pickups so the operator could see and hear what the waldo saw and heard. Still other controls fired the laser—or Fire Beam, as the Doimari called it.

"Don't the Fighting Machines have any other weapons than the Fire Beam?" asked Blade.

"No, curse it," said the woman. "We know they have throwers for fire bombs, like the ones the foot soldiers carry. But the throwers need a special kind of bomb, and we have found no such bombs in any city of the Land."

"That is unfortunate for the Seekers," said Blade. "If the Fighting Machines could throw their own bombs, they might not need the help of the men on foot. They could win the war by themselves."

The Seeker's eyes became still larger. "You think so?" Blade nodded. "Then perhaps we could ask that the war be put off, until we learned how to make the special bombs. . . ." Her voice trailed off, and she shook her head. "No. Feragga is too eager to begin the conquest of the Land. She would not allow it, and Nungor's friends would see it as weakness."

"Perhaps," said Blade and left the matter there. He hoped he'd sown a little more disagreement in Doimar, without giving the Doimari an idea they could use against Kaldak. He was going to have the same delicate problem time after time as long as he was in Doimar. He had to appear to be helpful without actually giving any help. He couldn't be sure of still being in this Dimension to help Kaldak defeat any schemes he'd suggested to the Doimari. Advising both sides in a war was fun in theory, but in practice it was more often than not a bloody headache!

Blade had to strip naked to use the control chair. As he did he was very aware of the woman's eyes roaming up and down his body. But she was still as thoroughly businesslike as Lord Leighton when it came time to get him hooked up.

The gloves and boots opened down the back, so they would fit almost any size of hand and foot, or at least almost any size of hand and foot in Doimar. Blade found them uncomfortably snug, although he could still move all his essential joints and muscles.

When the girl was sure of this, she pressed a green button on the frame. Blade heard a faint hum from the consoles, saw lights glowing on several of the consoles, and stood up. A second button made the chair swing back out of Blade's way. "All right, Blade. The Machine lives. Now start walking in place slowly, as if you'd just got up from being sick—no, no, not *that* slowly, you're not a baby!" and she clutched at her thick brown hair with both hands.

At the far end of the training room the waldo gave off a metallic squealing noise which set Blade's teeth on edge. Then slowly it started walking, with little shuffling steps very unlike the six-foot strides Blade knew the waldoes could take. He stopped, and it stopped, swaying so that for a moment Blade was afraid it would fall over. The Seeker winced. Then Blade cautiously turned his body to the left and started walking in place again. The waldo started off, this time heading for a point along the right wall of the room. Another stop, another turn, and it was heading to the left. Blade zig-zagged the waldo all the way down the training room until he could practically reach out and touch it, then sent it back to the far end and started all over again.

Within half an hour Blade felt confident he could make the robot do anything its mechanism could stand. After another half-hour, even the Seeker was convinced Blade knew how to handle the Fighting Machine safely. She cut off the power and showed Blade how the helmet worked.

"This mouthpiece is the basic control for the head and the laser. Bite down on the left end, and it turns the head. Bite down on the right, and it fires the laser. *Don't* get the two confused, or you might wind up killing yourself!"

Blade didn't kill himself, but he did take a chunk out of the wall of the training room by accident. Judging from the number of holes in the wall, he wasn't the first man to have such an accident. The woman made a great show of pounding her head against the consoles in frustration, but she was laughing as she did. Blade knew that he'd begun to impress her.

The video and audio systems had the same essential simplicity as the rest of the waldo. Padded earphones gave Blade stereo hearing, and padded eyepieces gave him a three-dimensional view complete with a sighting grid for aiming the laser. When Blade finally pulled off the helmet he was dripping sweat. He was also more than ever impressed with the technological gifts of the Tower Builders.

In fact he couldn't help wondering why they'd used these gifts to build the waldoes. They were an expensive and complicated way of getting armored firepower into battle. A remote-controlled tank would have been easier to build and probably more effective. The waldoes were deadly against any sort of primitive opponent, but they could hardly have been designed for action against one.

Not that Blade was unhappy with things as they were. A more effective kind of Fighting Machine would have meant a longer and harder war, with more dead among Doimar's enemies and more destruction in the Land. It might also have been harder for Doimar's enemies to learn to use, if they could find any in their own cities.

As it was, an intelligent child could almost learn to use one of the waldoes. The Seekers were talking nonsense when they spoke of their complexity, and Blade thought he knew why. They wanted to keep Nungor's infantrymen from realizing that almost anyone could use a waldo, and that the Seekers were basing their reputations on a lie. Blade wondered if he shouldn't reveal this secret to make real trouble between the two factions. Then he decided against it. He didn't know how many waldoes Doimar had. If it was only a hundred, it wouldn't make much difference how many men could use them. If it was a thousand, then increasing the number of men who could use them would make Doimar more powerful and dangerous.

On the other hand, if Kaldak could find some waldoes of its own, it would not take long for the Kaldakans to learn to use them. Blade knew that if he could get away and find waldoes in Kaldak, intelligent warriors like Sidas and Kareena would be using them effectively within a few weeks. Then Doimar's Fighting Machines would be meeting their own kind of battle, instead of walking over nearly helpless infantrymen.

113

Blade swung the seat back into place and sat down while the woman wiped him off with a towel. As she did, she chattered on about the problems of using the Fighting Machines without enough cooperation from Nungor's infantrymen.

"—all the sight and sound is much clearer here in the training room than out in the field. The Sky Voice reaches the Machines much more easily over short distances than over long ones."

"That must be why the Machine in Gilmarg did so poorly," said Blade helpfully. "The Voices were not reaching it clearly. The man in the chair could not see or hear clearly either."

The woman looked alarmed. "I hope you haven't told Nungor about the Machine's poor work."

This called for a polite lie. "Not yet. You think I should not?"

"Oh, yes, *please*. Knowing how poorly the Machine did will be a weapon for him against the Seekers. And it's all his fault that we can't take the Voice machines close to the battles."

She started massaging Blade's back and shoulders. It felt good but didn't take his mind off pumping the Seeker for more details. With only a little prompting, she told him practically everything he wanted to know, although he had to mentally translate many of the terms she used.

The Seekers knew they could not move the main control center for the waldoes. That was fixed in its underground complex three hundred feet below Doimar. They also knew enough about radio to understand the solution to the problem. If they had a network of mobile relay stations moving with the army, the radio signals (or "Voices") from the command center could reach and control waldoes all over the Land.

Unfortunately there was no way of moving Voice machines out of Doimar. "Can't you put them on munfans?" asked Blade.

She shook her head. "The strong Voice machines are too heavy to carry on munfans, and there is nothing else. There will be nothing else, thanks to Nungor, curse his black heart!"

"What has he done?"

"What hasn't he done, you mean? There are three whole rooms lager than this full of Oltec machines which could carry *anything* all over the Land. Not like the Fighting Machines, but other kinds, with wheels and other things. We of the Seekers could learn how to make them run, then carry voice machines into battle. It would be easy."

"But Nungor won't let you?"

"No! He says those machines belong to his army, the foot soldiers. He says this, and Feragga lets him say it, even though she knows the foot fighters have no knowledge of such machines. They talked about making the machines live someday, but they do not know how. Meanwhile the machines sit dead, while we who could make them live are not allowed near them." Her voice was getting shrill. "Nungor is like a dog who pisses on food he cannot eat himself." She leaned against Blade's back, shaking with rage or perhaps grief for her city.

"I am not surprised to hear this," said Blade quietly. "Nungor seems to be that sort of man. But maybe I can help you. Some of these machines might be like those I have used in England. If Nungor showed them to me, I might know how to make them live. After that, who could stop me from teaching the Seekers what I have learned? Not Nungor, certainly, and possibly not even Feragga." He smiled. "Of course the Seekers could not be too proud to learn from a stranger, but that—"

Her laughter held a slight note of hysteria. "Proud? Blade, I myself would eat dung if it would give us all the knowledge we must have. There are others who would do the same. If you can see the machines, and learn to use them. . . ." She sighed. "We will all be grateful." She ran her hands down Blade's chest and across his belly to his groin. "*I* will be grateful."

As Blade stood up, she peeled off her shirt and stood before him, naked to the waist. Her breasts were small but her nipples were large. As he soon discovered, they were also exquisitely sensitive. He used his fingers and lips on them until she was moaning happily even before they lay down together on a pile of clothing. Although she was small she lay down underneath, but his weight on top of

-115

her didn't keep her from thrashing wildly when she reached her climax.

Blade was glad he'd given her this much happiness, and with so little effort that he could keep half his thoughts on other matters. He didn't know what the other Oltec machines might be, but they certainly sounded worth investigating. They might even be the vehicles he and Kareena would need for a quick escape. He would still have to be careful not to teach Doimar too much. He would have to be even more careful in speaking to the ever-suspicious Nungor.

Blade turned back to the girl, and this time he gave their lovemaking all his attention.

Chapter 16

. Blade wasn't surprised by Nungor's reaction to his request, and he wasn't disappointed by the Oltec vehicles.

"The Seekers must have bought you," were Nungor's first words.

Blade shrugged. "You may say that if you wish. I will not take it as an insult, as I would have from a man of England. Yet I think you are not wise to say it, even though I will not have your blood for it."

"Why?"

"If the Seekers get any advantage from this, it will be your fault more than mine." Nungor's face set hard but Blade continued. "You did not say a single word to me about these vehicles. You left me ignorant until the Seekers chose to speak. If you had spoken first, I could have gone to see the vehicles with you many days ago. The Seekers would not have known anything until we finished our work and laid matters before Feragga. As it is, they will be watching and listening. This is *your* fault."

There was silence, while Blade mentally crossed his fingers. A strong attack was often the best defense in a situation like this, but he might have pushed Nungor too far. Certainly the man's fingers were twitching, as if they yearned to grip the hilt of his sword.

Then Nungor gave a quick, jerky nod. "All right. You make sense. We haven't had any luck with getting the machines to live ourselves. So we don't have anything to lose." He glared at Blade. "But don't breathe a word of how we failed to the Seekers. Otherwise Feragga herself won't be able to save you!"

"The Seekers will learn nothing from me," said Blade smoothly. It was a small concession to make, considering that the Seekers already knew practically everything about how the infantry had failed to make the Oltec vehicles run.

"Good. We'll go to the machine rooms tomorrow."

Each of the "machine rooms" was twice the size of the Seekers' training room for the waldoes. All three were filled with exotic military vehicles of at least twenty different kinds. They were parked in long rows on either side of wide aisles, which gave access to ramps leading to the surface at either end of the complex.

It looked like the vehicle park of an armored division whose vehicles were designed by madmen and assembled by drunks. Even the types of vehicles Blade could recognize at all were parodies of their Home Dimension counterparts. With others he couldn't even be sure what they were, let alone how they moved or how to operate them. Had the Tower Builders kept an experimental station in Doimar? Or had the last commander of the garrison before the war simply been part pack rat?

Trying to show more confidence than he felt, Blade lectured Nungor on the vehicles he thought he recognized or at least understood. The first one looked like the hull and turret of a small tank, but mounted on twelve stumpy articulated legs instead of on tracks.

"—not much use out of this unless there is ammunition for its weapon," he concluded. He couldn't tell what the

117

weapon was, although it didn't look like a gun, a laser, or a grenade launcher. "Also, you would need two or three men to make this one work in battle."

"You have said that the war machines of England use four or five men," Nungor pointed out. "Could you not teach the men of Doimar to do the same?"

"I could, if you gave me the time," said Blade. "I would have to teach each man his work, then teach each crew to work together. It might take as much as half a year. Do we have that much time?"

Nungor hesitated for a moment, clearly reluctant to reveal such a vital part of Doimar's war plans. Then he shook his head. "No. I would not even want to ask for it. Feragga would refuse it and not think well of either of us for asking."

"I thought so," said Blade. "Well, then we'll have to look at something else."

They spent the rest of a long day looking at one "something else" after another. Some vehicles Blade rejected because he couldn't even guess what they were, although he tried to hide his ignorance. One machine looked like a ferris wheel mounted on a tracked carriage twenty feet long and ten feet wide. Blade somehow doubted that the Tower Builders' army held carnivals for its men.

Blade rejected other machines because they were obviously no more than junk. Still others he rejected because they would be quite useless in Doimar's wars. A lot of engineering equipment fell into that category. Doimar's army wasn't going to build pontoon bridges, dig ditches, lay down fuel lines, or do many other engineering jobs a Home Dimension mechanized army faced in war.

Blade rejected some vehicles because he not only recognized them but knew they would be far too useful to Doimar and far too dangerous to Kaldak. There were a dozen or so tracked vehicles which could be nothing but armored personnel carriers. These could carry raiding parties of Doimari infantry deep into enemy territory. They could also carry the Seekers' radios, making the waldoes far more effective. Used either way they could mean disaster for Kaldak in the coming war.

Blade had to be particularly careful in explaining the

uselessness of the more useful vehicles. Nungor was no fool. Catching Blade in even a small lie might make him so suspicious that Blade's position—and Kareena's—would become impossible.

Fortunately Nungor's dislike of the Seekers did much of Blade's work for him. Most of the time Blade had only to mention that a certain vehicle might be useful to the infantry "—but would be far more useful to the Seekers, I'm afraid." Then Nungor would immediately start talking about ways of hiding this fact from the Seekers.

After a while he would always remember that this was hardly possible, as long as Feragga was sympathetic to the Seekers. Then he would finish with more or less the same words: "We'd better keep quiet about this one for a while."

Nungor might not be willing to see Doimar defeated rather than let the Seekers get the credit for a victory. But he was certainly willing to risk many things to reduce the Seekers' share of glory, including the lives of his own men. Blade was perfectly happy to encourage this desire. It not only made his own job of sabotaging Doimar's war effort a great deal easier, it made it considerably safer as well. If the Seekers and the infantry ever got together and compared notes on what Blade was telling them, he'd be finished. Thanks to Nungor's stubborn prejudices, that meeting would probably never take place.

They were halfway through the last room when Blade's eyes widened. The next six vehicles were identical—light Hovercraft with a large shrouded propeller in the rear and a domed passenger compartment in front. They didn't look heavily armed, so they were probably scout vehicles of some sort, relying on speed rather than firepower.

Nungor had noticed Blade's expression. "Ah, you think these are worth studying? So do we. We have even made one of them live for a short time." He pointed to the fourth Hovercraft.

"Why didn't you keep it alive?"

"We could make it rise and move. We could not make it move in one direction for long. It was like a wounded munfan running wild."

Blade nodded. Hovercraft could move fast and cross any sort of surface, but they were hard to steer. In a crosswind

119

it was almost impossible to keep them on a straight course, and even in a calm air they needed plenty of room to turn. Large Hovercraft like the ones used as ferries across the English Channel overcame the problem by sheer weight and power, but smaller machines simply needed careful handling.

Fortunately Blade was in a position to provide that careful handling. He'd learned to drive Hovercraft while taking his commando course with the Royal Marines. If the controls on the Tower Builders' machines were anything like those in Home Dimension . . . Blade hurried over to the fourth Hovercraft, scrambled up on the front, and peered in through the scratched and dusty windshield. A quick look was enough. He let out a shout of real pleasure, then dropped to the floor and hurried back to Nungor.

"Can you use this machine?" asked the War Captain.

Blade nodded. "We do not have such machines among the Oltec of England. But we did find books which spoke of them and how they were guided. I have read those books, and I think I can remember how to guide the machines. I will need a few days to practice, of course, and many large fire boxes to power the machines, but—"

"You can have anything you need, Blade, if—" Then he shook his head. "No. I must not promise too much. We shall have to get Ferraga's orders for what you need. She *will* insist that the Seekers learn of it, and then . . ." He sighed.

Blade grinned. "For once, this will make no difference. The Seekers will get no good from these machines, no matter how many we use." Nungor's mouth fell open and Blade continued smoothly. "To begin with, it will need strong and swift men and women to guide these machines. That means men and women like the foot soldiers, not like the weak and sickly Seekers." That did the Seekers an injustice, but it was what Nungor wanted to believe about them.

"Also, these machines cannot carry anything the Seekers need. They cannot carry the Fighting Machines or anything else heavy. They can easily carry foot soldiers or foot soldiers' weapons." That might even be the truth. The Hovercraft had a rear deck obviously able to hold cargo, but

120

they were certainly too small to lift a three-ton waldo. Blade was prepared to take his chances that they could not carry the radios.

"So—the foot soldiers will have this Oltec all to themselves, whatever Feragga says?"

"I do not know what Feragga will say," Blade pointed out. "She may try to favor the Seekers. But you can certainly trust me to speak strongly for the foot soldiers. Even Feragga of Doimar cannot make an Oltec machine into something it is not."

"No." Nungor was staring at the Hovercraft like a starving man offered a seven-course banquet. Blade practically had to drag him away. .

Like the other times Blade dined with Feragga, this meal ended with a huge bowl of fruit sliced up in honey. As usual, Feragga served herself the lion's share of the bowl. The chief of Doimar had a sweet tooth.

As she spooned up the dessert with childish pleasure, Blade watched the candlelight play on Feragga's smooth brown skin, showing the muscles rippling under it. There was more skin than usual on display tonight. Feragga wore her knee-length boots with knives in them, a skirt of blue leather reaching to her ankles but slit up to one hip, and nothing else except a heavy dose of perfume. The perfume could not entirely hide Feragga's reluctance to take a bath more than once a week.

Otherwise Blade had to admit that the less Feragga wore the better she looked. Her breasts were large, in proportion to the rest of her, but well shaped and solid. The curve of her belly told of muscle rather than flab, and her surprisingly graceful throat—

Blade realized he was staring at her a moment before Feragga laughed. "Ah, Blade. Sometimes I think I should bed you. Sometimes I think I should not. Sometimes I think I should ask you to decide for me. But if you are going to look at me like that, I know the answer you would give if I asked. So perhaps I should not trust you that much in matters where your prick might rule you."

She pushed the empty dish away, lit a fresh candle from the dying one, and signaled to the maidservant at the door to leave them. When the door closed, Feragga's smile faded. "You are wiser in matters of war and Oltec, I think. So there I will trust you." She filled both their cups with beer from a jug on the floor beside her. "Nungor says you can make one of the Oltec carrying machines live again. Is this so?"

"If he says that I am sure of it, he is hoping for too much," began Blade cautiously. "If he says that I think I can learn the machine's ways, then teach them to others . . ." He shrugged. "I will not give you false hopes, Feragga."

"Good. I would not thank you for that." She gulped her beer noisily. "Nungor also says that the Seekers cannot use these machines."

Blade nodded. "There he says what I think, too. I know the Seekers' wisdom and do not think they lack courage. But I do not know what they could do with these machines. If I knew more of the Seekers' work—"

Feragga raised a hand. "You shall, Blade. You shall, as soon as you have learned how to guide these machines. You shall teach the Seekers as well as the footmen how to guide them. In return the Seekers will tell you *everything* they know."

"Thank you, Feragga. This will make my work easier. But—will Nungor—"

Feragga slammed her cup down on the table hard enough to knock spoons and knives off onto the floor. "I piss in Nungor's beer! He will like it, or I will find another War Captain. For too long the Seekers and the footmen have been fighting like tomcats. The Doimari will never rule the Land if we go on running off in different directions like a flock of sheep when a greathawk swoops down!" She poured herself more beer. "But with your help, Blade, this can change."

"I will be glad to help," said Blade. He was still cautious. In spite of her coarse manners, Feragga was dangerously sensible. She might ask him to do something which would be fatal to Kaldak.

"Good." She explained. Once he'd proved he could make the Oltec vehicles live again, Blade would be named Doimar's Captain of Oltec, ranking equal to both the First Seeker and Nungor the War Captain. He would be given a staff of intelligent men and women, chosen equally from the Seekers and from the foot soldiers. With this staff, he would find, study, and learn to use any Oltec found in the cities Doimar conquered. Then he would teach what he'd learned to *both* the Seekers and the foot soldiers.

"How many people will I have under me?" Blade asked. So far, the plan didn't seem to present any immediate danger to Kaldak, but he wanted to be sure. "If I'm going to have to search each city in the Land from tower top to cellar—"

Feragga laughed, spraying beer into Blade's face. "Don't worry, Blade. We've got maps of at least a dozen of the cities, showing where all the Oltec is hidden. Those Law-bound fools have been sitting on treasures for centuries. That proves how unfit they are to hold it. In Doimar we've gone beyond the Law, and that proves we're the destined rulers of the Land!" Feragga seemed to be feeling the beer.

"You didn't have a map of Gilmarg, did you?" said Blade. He was fishing for more information about those maps.

Feragga grunted like a pig. "No, worse luck. If we had, we'd have stripped that storeroom empty long before you led the Kaldakans to it. Oh, well, we'll dig up that building you dropped on it someday, and we've got plenty of other maps." She laughed. "Would you believe we even have one of Kaldak?"

"I'll believe it if I see it," said Blade, trying hard to make a joke of the matter.

"You will, you will. You might as well start studying those maps while you're studying the machines. You've got to have something to do at night besides take slave girls to bed." She punched Blade in the shoulder. "I'm not jealous. I know you've got enough manhood to have some left for me. So don't look so worried about that."

Blade wasn't looking worried. He was trying desperately to hide his excitement. Feragga was offering him a map showing all Kaldak's hidden Oltec! That could save months in preparing the city for war, if he could get back there

123

with the information. From now on, that was going to have to be his main goal—that, and making sure Kareena was not left to die horribly.

Feragga reached across the table, gripped Blade by both shoulders, and pulled him toward her as easily as if he'd been a child. He wound up with his face buried between her breasts. Then she ruffled his hair with one hand and kissed him on the forehead. It was rather like being kissed by an affectionate bear.

"This won't be our night, Blade," she said. "When you've done your work with the machines—ah, that will be the time. We can celebrate making you Captain of Oltec properly. Good night and skilled hands."

The ritual wish for anyone working with Oltec was Blade's dismissal. He left quickly, trying to stagger convincingly as if he'd drunk more than he actually had. It would do no harm if Feragga thought he was too drunk to remember all she'd said to him.

It would do even less harm if she kept her promise not to take him to bed until he'd finished his work with the Hovercraft. If she did it before then Nungor's jealousy could still wreck everything. If she waited, Blade didn't plan to be in Doimar, let alone ready to warm her bed.

He and Kareena would be either dead or on their way home to Kaldak.

Chapter 17

For the next few weeks, Blade would have been happier if he'd been triplets. There was too much for any one man to do. Fortunately Blade knew what to do in this sort of situation. He sat down and divided all the work into what absolutely *had* to be done before he left Doimar, dead or alive, and what it would be merely *useful* to do. That shrank the work down to what one man could do, as long as the man had the constitution of a horse and the ability to go for weeks on end with three hours' sleep a night. Blade qualified. Otherwise he'd have been dead years ago.

By day Blade practiced with the Hovercraft, not only operating it but also learning to maintain and repair it. He knew this could possibly give the Doimari knowledge they would afterward use against Kaldak. On the other hand, Blade needed the knowledge to be reasonably sure of escaping. The Sky Masters built their machinery to last, but the Hovercraft was still centuries old. It would do him and Kareena no good if it broke down ten miles outside Doimar.

The controls of the Hovercraft were so simple that Blade could operate it without being able to read the instruments Unlike the waldoes, though, the Hovercraft was nothing for a child to handle. Even Blade needed all his training and reflexes to control it at high speed. He felt as if he was driving a sports car across slick ice, and didn't even try to push the Hovercraft to its limits. It would easily buzz along at eighty miles an hour, and at that speed it would leave everything in this Dimension far behind, including the waldoes.

The Hovercraft was designed on the modular system. When something broke, you simply pulled the whole piece out and shoved in a new one. With five other Hovercraft to cannibalize for parts, Blade had no trouble getting the sixth into nearly perfect condition. He also hoped to immobilize the other five by stealing parts from them. The Hovercraft could easily carry the radios the Seekers needed for their relay system. If none of the Hovercraft left behind ever moved again, it would be much safer for Kaldak.

That was Blade's day. Most of his nights were spent studying the maps of the cities of the land. He secretly made two copies of the map of Kaldak and hid each one in a different place in his suite. Then he set himself to the task of memorizing the locations of all the Oltec storerooms under Kaldak, so that if he had to escape without the maps the information still wouldn't be lost. When he wanted it that way, Blade's memory was nearly photographic.

The nights he didn't spend studying maps were spent making love to slave girls or sometimes free women of Doimar. Rumors of his silver loinguard were spreading, and many women seemed convinced that the penis it protected must be something special. Blade was always willing to do his best to prove the point, as amusing as he found the notion. Very few women seemed to go away unsatisfied.

In fact, it was the kind of satisfaction Blade gave some of them which brought on the crisis.

Another blood-red sunset was tinting Doimar outside Blade's window. Another company of infantry was training in the courtyard three hundred feet below. This time they were practicing hand-grenade throwing. Blade heard sharp explosions as the grenades went off behind walls of piled earth and stone. Sometimes he heard screams as a grenade went off prematurely in someone's hand. If Blade hadn't known already that the armies of Doimar were going to march soon, the training he'd seen these past few days would have convinced him. Nungor and Feragga didn't seem to care if they killed a third of their infantry as long as the other two-thirds were properly trained.

Blade decided to treat himself to a good night's sleep for once. There were no women coming tonight, the Hovercraft was about as ready as it ever would be, and he'd memorized all the information about Kaldak's Oltec anyone was likely to need during the war. He drew a cup of beer from the barrel in the corner of the bedroom, drank it, then started taking off his clothes.

He'd stripped down to the loinguard when he heard the sound of many feet shuffling outside the door. Then he heard a furious knocking, with fists, spear butts, sword hilts, and clubs. It sounded as if the people out there were rioters who wanted to break down the door. He grabbed his sword but didn't worry about his clothes.

Feragga's voice cut through the din outside. "Stop it, you fools! I wouldn't blame him if he killed the first half-dozen if you burst in on him this way!" Blade smiled. He'd been planning to do exactly that if the Doimari had come to arrest him. Apparently they hadn't—or at least Feragga hadn't.

Her voice came again. "Blade, we mean you no harm. But we must have your silver loinguard."

"My—silver loinguard?" said Blade. He wasn't playing for time; he was honestly confused.

"Yes. Seven of the women you have taken to your bed are with child. Seven! No man in the memory of Kaldak has done so well in his whole life. You have done this in less than a month. We must have your loinguard to study, to know if it holds your secret!"

Blade laughed. "I have said the secret is in me, not in the loinguard. Do you doubt my word, Feragga?"

"I do not doubt that you are telling the truth as far as you know it, Blade. But do you know everything? The Seekers doubt it and would like to study the loinguard itself. Now may they have it peacefully?" She left the implied threat unspoken, but Blade heard the rasp of swords being drawn.

If he gave up the loinguard, there'd be practically no chance of his ever seeing it again. One of Lord Leighton's key experiments would lack its final results, and the scientist would not be happy, to put it mildly. The work of getting a protective garment for Blade—and possibly another traveler—to take into Dimension X would be set back. The Seekers might even learn enough from the loinguard to develop some suspicions about Blade's origins.

Yet they could hardly deduce the whole Dimension X secret from one piece of strange alloy. Nothing short of the Dimension X secret itself was worth the trouble Blade would face if he didn't give up the loinguard. The Doimari were obviously prepared to take it by force. They might not want to kill the goose who laid the golden eggs—or in this case, the gander with the golden loins. But accidents could happen, and in any case Kareena might be horribly punished for his stubbornness. At best, he would probably be put under guard like a stud stallion, and his chances of escaping would practically disappear.

"All right," he said loudly enough to be heard by everyone outside. "I give up my badge of a warrior of England for the good of Doimar. But it is unseemly for a warrior of England to be without his badge, so I must ask you to return it to me in five days' time." Blade didn't know if they would agree to this condition, but he had nothing to lose by asking and everything to gain. He'd be able to make his getaway as he had planned and still return to Home Dimension with the silver loinguard.

There was no sound out in the hallway for a few seconds, then Blade heard Feragga's voice. "All right, Blade, we agree to return it to you in five days' time. Now let's have it."

"There's just one more thing," Blade said. "Let me get some clothes on. Then I will let you in." He was damned if he'd face the crowd out there in his bare skin. His private parts were *not* going to be on public display for the Doimari.

Feragga and Nungor led the crowd into the room. Blade handed the loinguard to Feragga, who handed it to Rehna, the Seeker woman who'd trained Blade in using the waldoes. She looked so unhappy that Blade drew Feragga aside and asked why.

"Rehna has not conceived from your seed," said Feragga. She sighed. "Yet she has had you in her, and she may have another chance. Consider *my* situation. Now I cannot bed you at all, for I am certainly past bearing children if I ever could. Your seed is abundant, to be sure, but you do not have enough to waste on dried-up old husks like me." There was real pain in her voice.

Blade kissed her gently, ignoring Nungor's frown. "Do not call yourself harsh names, Feragga. There will be a time when duty is done and pleasure is our right. Meanwhile, you are the mother of all Doimar. You have twenty thousand children, and that is more than I will ever sire."

Blade was glad to see Feragga smile, because his praise was almost sincere. Like too many rulers he'd met, Feragga was cruel, ruthless, and ambitious for power and conquest. Unlike some, she was not mad. Confronted with a Kaldak armed, able to defend itself, she might see reason and make peace. Then the work of Doimar's Seekers would in the long run benefit everyone in the Land.

However, she was still going to have to be defeated first.

Blade quickly discovered that in fact he was going to be kept in a gilded stall as Doimar's prize stud stallion, even though he'd given up the loinguard peacefully. He would

128

have every luxury Doimar could supply and a different woman each night. He would also have very little privacy and therefore not much chance of escaping.

"You look worried, Blade," said Feragga, when she'd finished explaining how he'd be treated. "Does any of this go against the Law of England? I would not have suspected you were the sort of Law-bound fool to think of such things."

"I am not," said Blade firmly. "You should know that by now. It is entirely Lawful for a warrior of England to give his seed to women of other lands, and even leave his children in them. But if I am to do this as you wish, I must have two things."

"If they are in Doimar, you may have them," said Nungor.

"Good. One is five days to go through certain rites. It is the custom of England for a man to perform them before he goes to his bride. They are said to increase his powers both to please women and to give them children." Five days should be enough to finish his work with the Hovercraft and stock it with food, water, weapons, and spare power cells for the escape—not to mention getting the loinguard back.

"We are glad to honor the customs of England," said Feragga. "What is the second thing?"

"I would like to have Kareena, daughter of Peython, here as my slave, to begin her Initiation and—"

"You don't mean to put your seed into her?" said Nungor sharply. "She is not worthy to bear children who will be the strength of Doimar."

Apparently Nungor's suspicions weren't being lulled by the fact that Feragga was no longer planning to take Blade to bed. The man was simply suspicious by nature.

Feragga glared at Nungor and opened her mouth, but Blade spoke first. "Nungor, your tongue runs ahead of your wits. I have said nothing about giving seed to Kareena. I wish her to do some useful work as part of her Initiation, by keeping these rooms clean, waiting on the women I take to bed, and so on. If she has her strength back, it is time we put that strength to use. Like my seed, it should not be wasted."

He let an edge creep into his voice. "And if I did wish to put my seed into Kareena, Peython's daughter, I would do so. You could not stop me. I would not call her unworthy to bear sons for any city. She is Peython's daughter, and although he fears the Law too much I have not heard that he is weak, foolish, or a coward. Neither is his daughter." Blade caught his breath, realizing that he might have put himself and Kareena in danger but not caring too much. He'd be damned if he was going to kiss Nungor's arse forever!

Feragga gave one of her robust laughs. "Blade, you have said what I was going to say better than I could have said it myself. Certainly you can have Kareena to serve you. When you have taken all the women of Doimar who will share your bed, you can even put your seed into her if you have any left. Indeed, a child of Peython's daughter will not be unworthy of Doimar. When do you want Kareena brought here?"

"Oh, in a day or two will be soon enough," said Blade with elaborate casualness. "I would like to teach her some of her duties before I start entertaining the ladies of Doimar every night."

"It shall be done," said Nungor, his face and voice both expressionless.

The last of the guards rolled off Kareena and rejoined his fellows standing around her. He didn't bother looking at her, let alone try to help her to her feet. She lay on the filthy straw until she felt she could stand up easily. She would not let these swine see her struggling to her feet, let alone ask one of them for help.

Gradually what strength she had left returned to her limbs. She was able to sit, then stand up. No one made a move to offer her any clothing, but she would have been surprised if they had. She'd been naked most of the time since they carried her out of the room where Blade stood, calmly betraying Kaldak to that bitch Feragga!

Blade! The mere thought of his name nauseated her. She would have vomited if there'd been anything in her stomach. She hated him more than any of the Doimari guards who'd made her their plaything for the past weeks. They were hardly more than animals. Blade knew what he was doing.

A sharp pain in her leg made her bite her ragged lips and lean against the wall of the cell for a moment. She could stand and even walk slowly, but not much more. The leg would probably never be completely right again. Once the thought of spending the rest of her life walking with a limp would have been agony. That time now seemed long ago, in the life of a person other than the Kareena who now stood naked in a filthy cellar in Doimar.

More guards were coming now, bringing one of those metal chairs they used to carry her. She started walking over to it herself. She would not give them any excuse to manhandle her, not when the bruises from the last beating hadn't healed yet, and she would certainly be getting fresh ones when she got to wherever they were taking her. That had been the rule—a beating every time she was moved. At least they hadn't used the iron-tipped Initiation whip. She'd seen what that did and knew it might have broken her.

The guards lifted the chair and trotted down the hall, then turned right and stopped before a tall metal door. To Kareena's surprise it slid open, revealing one of the elevators. Where was she going, that they were taking her there by elevator? As far as she knew, the elevators only worked in Feragga's tower and one or two others in all of Doimar.

The elevator lurched upward, creaking and hissing, for quite a while. When the door opened again Kareena saw the guards outside wore Feragga's house badge. She was in the bitch-chief's tower. Then she saw something which drove all thoughts of Feragga out of her mind.

Blade was standing behind the guards, arms crossed on his massive chest. He looked as she'd expected him to look—clean, well-fed, self-satisfied, and as arrogant as if he ruled here instead of Feragga. Then he started giving orders, as if he took it for granted that he'd be obeyed.

"Bring hot water and soap and give Kareena a bath. Clean her wounds, rub her with oil, and give her a meal with some *meat* in it."

"And the chain, Blade?" asked the chief of the guards carrying the chair.

"To be sure, the chain. But make it a long one, and

131

wrap the leg iron in cloth. She'll have a lot of work to do, so I want her to be able to move about the rooms."

"As you command, Blade."

In front of Blade, Kareena was suddenly self-conscious about her nakedness for the first time since reaching Doimar. She wanted to cover her face or her breasts with her hands. Instead she forced herself to raise her head and stare hard at him. For a moment he stared back, then he looked sharply away.

She knew that he hadn't looked away because he was ashamed: clearly he felt nothing for her. He'd only ordered the bath and the meal because he didn't want a filthy, starved scarecrow of a slave in his comfortable rooms. Angrily she told her stomach to stop rumbling at the thought of meat, the first she would be tasting since she reached Doimar.

Perhaps Blade felt guilty over betraying Kaldak. He certainly should, by the Lords of the Law! But that wouldn't save him, either. If she was on a long chain, she would have a chance to explore his rooms when he wasn't around. There should be something she could hide, then use as a weapon at the right time.

The time would surely come. He'd want to bed her, if only to humiliate her. He'd be lost in rut then, and she would still be clear and cool in her mind and body. She'd be able to pick her moment, then strike to avenge her own honor and that of her city.

Perhaps she could kill that piece of dung Blade outright. If she could do that, she wouldn't care what they did to her afterward. She could certainly take his eyes or his manhood or perhaps both. After that she might have the chance to end her own life.

She'd thought sometimes of doing that in the prison. She'd even had opportunities. Now she knew that nothing would make her turn against herself before she tried to strike at Blade. Now she knew she might not die dishonored and degraded but in a way worthy of Peython's daughter and a warrior of Kaldak. She could almost feel grateful to Blade, that his death or mutilation would give her back her own honor.

Chapter 18

Rehna fell asleep soon after reaching her climax. Blade waited until her even breathing told him she was dead to the world, then cautiously shifted his position to look at Kareena. She lay on her pallet by the window, her knees drawn almost up to her breasts and her hair streaming across the pillow. Sometimes she whimpered or twitched in the grip of nightmares. She'd kicked off the blankets and the moonlight silvered her body, giving it back some of the beauty she'd lost during her captivity.

You'll have it all back, Kareena. All of it, or you'll be past suffering. He wished he could have spared her the final degradation of being here while he made love to Rehna, but Feragga had been insistent that Blade's stud service begin on schedule. The thought made him turn back to Rehna.

Now there was a smile on her small face. Blade was glad he'd been able to make her the first woman he took to his bed "officially." He hoped she would conceive by him, and not just because he knew that would make her even happier. Carrying his child would also help protect her from Feragga's or Nungor's anger after his escape.

Meanwhile, there were a few other things he could do to protect her. Quietly he sought her carotid artery and applied pressure with his thumbs. In a few moments Rehna was not just asleep but unconscious. Blade made sure she was still breathing, then slipped out of bed and started pulling on his clothes. At intervals he spared a look for Kareena. She was still asleep, but now she'd stretched out on her back, one hand under her head and the other out of sight under the pillow.

At last Blade was fully dressed and armed. He was wearing the loinguard once again, the Seekers having returned it to him that morning after determining it had no secret powers. The two maps of Kaldak were snugly hidden away in different pockets. He walked over to the head of Kareena's pallet, bent down, and whispered.

"Kareena, wake up. We're going to escape."

Only Blade's quick reflexes saved him from death or at least from losing an eye. Kareena's hand came out from under the pillow like a striking rattlesnake, and there was a long sharp piece of wire in it. The end of the wire struck where Blade's throat would have been if he hadn't already been moving. She struck again, opening a gash in his forehead just above his left eye, then he chopped down on her wrist so hard that her fingers went limp and the wire dropped to the floor.

"Kareena, stop it! We're *escaping,* I said!" He'd half-expected this, but nothing had prepared him for the sheer ugliness of Kareena's expression. She looked like a madwoman, and the nails of her usable hand clawed at his face. He felt more blood flow, saw her open her mouth to scream, and knew there was only one thing to do. He clamped one hand over her mouth, gritted his teeth as she bit it to the bone, then applied the same pressure he'd used on Rehna. After an impossibly long time she went limp and those mad eyes closed.

Kareena's being a dead weight was going to slow him down at a time when every moment counted, but the idea of leaving her behind never occurred to Blade. They were both going to be out of Doimar tonight, either dead or alive. Blade picked up Rehna's clothing and pulled it onto Kareena as well as he could. It was a poor fit, since Kareena was a good real taller than the Seeker. It still made Kareena look enough like a Seeker to fool anyone who didn't look too closely or saw her in poor light. Since the halls of Feragga's tower were hardly lit at night and the guards were usually half-asleep, Blade thought there was a chance.

It was the work of a minute to unlock Kareena's leg

iron. He spent another minute tearing Kareena's blankets into strips and tying Rehna hand and foot. Then he lifted Kareena over one shoulder, her legs down his back and her hair falling over her face. With most of her bruises hidden, she looked rather like a Seeker who'd drunk too much while Blade was entertaining her. In spite of being half-starved, she was also heavy enough to make Blade glad he'd already hidden most of his equipment in the Hovercraft.

Kareena's disguise got her and Blade past the first four sets of guards and safely out of Feragga's tower. They were halfway to the vehicle building when two more guards loomed out of the darkness. Blade recognized them as two of Nungor's picked men, and probably briefed by their suspicious chief. He decided that against these two a surprise offense was the best defense.

"Good evening, men," he said cheerfully, striding up to them. "I'm trying to get this lady home without anyone being the wiser. If you fellows will help me and keep quiet about it, you'll be a good deal richer."

One of the men laughed coarsely. "Poking her out of her proper turn, eh? All right. It's no harm done to us, whatever Feragga may say." He looked at her robe. "A Seeker, eh? If she lives in the Seekers' tower we've a good walk ahead of us. Let me take a turn carrying her."

"Thank you." Blade handed Kareena to the first guard, while the second turned his back to keep watch. The moment the first guard's hands were filled with Kareena, Blade drew his sword and slashed the second guard across the back of the neck. He'd kept the edge razor-sharp and the steel went through flesh and spine as if it were straw. The guard was dead before he could even start to fall.

The guard holding Kareena was frozen with surprise for a decisive second. Blade wheeled on one foot and kicked the man in the groin with the other. He dropped Kareena to the rocky ground and doubled up, his face a death-mask and both hands clutching his ruined manhood. He made no effort to defend himself as Blade chopped him across the throat with the edge of one hand. He only fell down and lay on his side, gasping and choking until his breath rattled to a stop and the life went out of him.

135

Blade quickly checked Kareena for injuries. She was unhurt, except for a few new cuts, and still unconscious, but her Seeker's robe was too badly ripped to be much of a disguise any more. However, there were replacements ready to hand. Blade dragged both guards into the shelter of a ruined building and started stripping them.

When he lifted Kareena again, she was wearing the first guard's clothing. He himself was carrying a laser rifle and two grenades as well as a second sword. He still wasn't in a position to fight his way through serious opposition, entirely apart from the danger of waking the whole city. He was no longer largely at the mercy of Kareena's disguise and his own ability to lie.

Blade ducked and dodged through the streets of Doimar to the vehicle building. When it finally came in sight, he stopped and felt like cursing. At the entrance to one of the ramps from the vehicle rooms, four guards sat around a small fire. Four guards, where normally there was only one sentry walking back and forth.

Maybe it was Nungor's suspicions, maybe it was just a precaution now that war was so close. Either way it was bad news for Blade. He wasn't going to be able to bluff his way through four guards. If anything went wrong it would be almost impossible to deal with all of them before either he or Kareena got badly hurt.

Fortunately there was a simpler method of dealing with the guards. Blade put Kareena down, unslung the rifle, put a fresh power cell into it, then lay down in the shadow of a building. The moment all four guards were properly grouped, he opened fire. His first shot took the leader in the face and he fell sideways into the fire with his mouth still open. The fire's going out made the other guards harder to see, but not that much harder to hit. Laser weapons light up their own targets. Blade killed all three before any of them could give the alarm, although he had to use three shots to do away with the last man. Then he snatched up Kareena, sprinted across the open ground, and plunged down the ramp.

Halfway down the ramp Blade felt Kareena starting to wriggle. Without breaking stride he whispered savagely, "Keep still, you crazy bitch! We're halfway done already!

If you bugger things up now—!" She understood the tone if not the words and went limp again. She stayed that way until Blade reached his chosen Hovercraft. As he laid her down in one of the two couches in front of the control panel, she opened her eyes.

For the moment Blade had no time for her. He darted through the interior of the Hovercraft, inspecting his cached supplies. The bottled water and emergency rations were still there, although in a pinch he'd have been prepared to leave without them and take his chances on living off the land. The crate of hand grenades and the extra power cells were another matter. Without the first they might not be able to fight their way clear of Doimar, and without the second they certainly couldn't hope to reach Kaldakan territory.

Everything was in place. Blade brought the grenades forward and put the open crate on the floor between the two control couches. As he straightened up, he felt Kareena's eyes on him. For the first time in months, he was able to meet them.

After a moment she licked her lips. "Blade—are those men back there—dead?"

He snorted. "If they aren't, it's not my fault."

"You—killed them?"

"You don't tickle people with a laser rifle!"

She shook her head as if stinging insects were swarming around her face and blinked. "Then—we *are* escaping?"

"Of course." Blade resisted the temptation to add, "And we'd have been on our way long before this if you hadn't made me put you to sleep!" He had a fairly good idea of what she'd been through, and more harsh words were the last thing she needed now. Instead he held out a grenade to her. "You know how to use these?"

"Yes. Pull the ring on top, then throw it."

"Yes. Or hold it against yourself, if you're about to be captured. That way you'll die quickly and maybe take a few Doimari with you as well." He pulled out one of the maps of Kaldak and handed it to Kareena. "Take this, too, in case we get separated. It's a map showing all the rooms full of Oltec under Kaldak."

Kareena stared. "Thank you, Blade—I think. I'm begin-

ning to believe this isn't a dream." She squeezed her eyes
shut, obviously fighting back tears. He patted her hand,
saw her flinch, and decided not to touch her again. It
might be years before a man's touch didn't repel her, and if
so this would be partly his fault.

However, feeling guilty never won any battles and might
lose this one. Their escape was no longer a dream, but it
might easily turn into a nightmare if he didn't get the Hovercraft moving soon.

Blade took several deep breaths, then sent his hands
dancing over the controls without bothering to turn on the
cabin lights. He'd memorized all the essential controls until
he could use them in the dark. The motor started, then the
fans whined into life. The Hovercraft started to shudder,
then Blade fed more power to the fans at the same time as
he cut in the propeller. In a single smooth movement the
Hovercraft rose from the concrete and slid forward into the
aisle.

Blade immediately learned that he wasn't as calm as
he'd thought. He nearly ran the Hovercraft into an armored personnel carrier across the aisle before he could get
it turned around. *Slow and steady, Blade, slow and steady,*
he told himself. *This isn't the place to use the Hovercraft's
speed.* He knew that most of his unusual nervousness came
from the woman sitting beside him. He also knew that nervousness would do her no good at all. He took more deep
breaths.

Then the Hovercraft was heading straight down the
aisle. They passed through the doorway into the next room
and down its aisle, until the ramp to the surface appeared
ahead. Blade gave the propeller more power as they hit the
ramp. Then five more guards appeared at the top of the
ramp, two of them with their lasers already raised.

"Down, Kareena!" Blade roared. He flung the Hovercraft up the ramp straight at the guards, wishing he had a
machine gun mounted in the bow. He needn't have worried. The sight of the Hovercraft charging them was
enough to defeat the guards. They scattered without firing,
although not before one pulled the pin out of a grenade and
dropped it on the concrete. It rolled down the ramp and
went off abreast of the Hovercraft. The machine leaped

and the roof of the cabin struck the roof of the vehicle building so violently that the top hatch was torn away.

Blade fought the machine back under control as the roar of the wind and the whine of the propeller and fans filled the cabin. Then he saw Kareena pulling herself painfully up to the open hatch with one hand, holding the grenade in the other. In the best war-movie tradition she pulled the pin with her teeth, then pitched the grenade into the middle of the fleeing guards. As the explosion cut them down she practically fell back into the cabin, her face pale but her teeth bared in a positively devilish grin.

"That was a foolish thing to do," said Blade. He would have said something stronger, but he needed all his concentration to steer the Hovercraft past the mangled remains of the guards. If a large piece got caught in the lift fans—!

"You wouldn't think so, if you'd been stinking and hurt down where I was as long as I was," she said sharply. "And I won't take any more orders from you. You can't knock me out again, either."

"Then what are you going to do, Kareena?" The last of the guards' remains was behind them now, but they were still a good distance from the open streets, let alone the open countryside.

She laughed grimly. "I won't kill you. I promise you that. Or at least I won't kill you until you've helped me kill at least a few more Doimari."

"All right," said Blade. He steered for a moment with one hand, while handing her the laser rifle with the other. "Just don't shoot off our own propeller. I don't particularly want to get killed at all, but I'd rather be killed by you than by the Doimari!"

She laughed again. At least they seemed to agree on something. Blade concentrated on getting the Hovercraft onto a main street. The moment he found one leading the right way, he gave the Hovercraft almost full power. The staring faces of the few people abroad at night turned into white blurs. Gravel rattled like shotgun blasts on the hull and once Blade heard the whipcrack of a laser. The fans and propeller still whined as steadily as if they were fresh from the factory.

The Hovercraft was doing at least sixty miles an hour

when it hit the Loga River to the south of Doimar. It went halfway across before Blade got it under control, but that was an advantage. Now they were out of rifleshot from the city, and he doubted if there were any mortars or waldoes alerted yet. He straightened the Hovercraft out and accelerated again, ignoring the cloud of spray which nearly blocked the view ahead. Out here on the open river they had plenty of room.

The Hovercraft was hitting nearly seventy miles an hour when the last lights of Doimar disappeared in the darkness behind it. Blade slowed down to take his bearings, then absent-mindedly bent over to kiss Kareena. Instantly her eyes flared open and her hands turned into claws. Blade suspected that even now he'd lose an eye if he touched her. "Get some sleep, Kareena," he said roughly, then turned back to the controls.

He didn't blame her for looking at him that way, and he wondered why he cared so much that she did. Nonetheless he knew that if the light didn't come back into her eyes before he left this Dimension he would feel his victory was incomplete.

Blade, you are getting much too soft in the heart or the head or both for this kind of work.

Lord Leighton would tell him that. Even J might do the same. But neither of them would ever have to meet Kareena's haunted eyes.

Chapter 19

Blade kept the Hovercraft on the river until dawn, following the route he'd planned after looking at the Doimari maps of the Land. The shortest route home to Kaldak lay through rough country. The Hovercraft might not be able to get through at all, and it would certainly be slowed down so much that the Doimari pursuers might catch up.

So Blade was taking the long way home, down the Loga River which flowed past Doimar to Lake Mison, across the lake, and then over the plains to the south of the lake into Kaldakan territory. As the crow flies, it was three times as long as the other route, but the Hovercraft wasn't a crow. On the water or on the plains Blade could use its speed freely.

There were still dangers, of course. If the Hovercraft broke down or ran out of power, Blade and Kareena would be a long way from home. Before they could walk back to Kaldak, the war might be over and Kaldak no more than a mass of smoking ruins.

A second danger on this route was the Tribes. Doimar had no settlements more than fifty miles downriver, and no city at all claimed the shores of Lake Mison. The Tribes roamed there freely, fishing, hunting, and fighting with each other. They sometimes respected the power of the cities' armies enough to leave their citizens alone, and sometimes killed them on sight. Blade hoped they could avoid the Tribes entirely. He and Kareena would be around Lake Mison for only a day or two, so their chances would be good.

Blade sent the Hovercraft racing down the Loga with an easy mind. Beside him Kareena gradually fell asleep in her couch, while the sky to the east turned gray with the coming dawn.

By the time it was full daylight, they'd reached the mouth of the Loga. Lake Mison stretched out before them, so wide at this point it was impossible to see the far bank. The rising wind was also kicking up whitecapped waves four or five feet high.

Reluctantly Blade decided against taking the Hovercraft out to one of the small islands in the middle of the lake. They'd be safer from the Tribes there, but they'd also have to battle the waves. Even if they didn't run into trouble on the way, they might find themselves stranded on the island until the wind died.

He turned the Hovercraft onto the hard beach running

south from the mouth of the river and increased speed again. Kareena woke up, asked what he was doing, listened to his explanation, and fell asleep again. Blade was happy to leave her alone. Sleep would be better for her than anything he could do now.

Blade headed south along the lakeshore until he was sure they were far beyond any territory the Doimari ever visited. Then he ran the Hovercraft up onto the grassy hillside above the beach, cut the power, and woke Kareena. She shook herself, climbed out, and stood in the long grass. The wind from the lake sent her hair streaming out behind her. Blade alternated between watching her and heating some emergency rations on the hotplate under the control panel. Otherwise he was prepared to wait, then listen to whatever she would say to him whenever she wanted to say it. Only after that would it make any sense for him to speak.

The hours of Kareena's silence still tested Blade more than some of the battles he'd fought. She moved around as stiff-limbed as a wooden puppet, her mouth tightly shut but her eyes wide and staring. It looked as though she wouldn't believe she was safely out of Doimar until she'd taken in every detail of the landscape. She drank some water but refused to eat or show an unnecessary inch of skin. She kept her boots on and made a hood for her face out of a spare piece of cloth. She even insisted on walking a hundred yards away from the Hovercraft to empty her bladder. Blade didn't care for her taking that risk, and said so.

"The Tribesmen are thinly scattered, but we don't know where they might pop up. So why take chances?"

Kareena said nothing in reply—at least nothing in words. Instead her mask broke again and a wild animal looked out at Blade. By sheer reflex he took two steps backward and dropped into karate stance. Before he could recover, Kareena was walking off into the grass. He didn't waste his breath chasing her or even shouting. She wouldn't hear words, and if he chased her she might break completely and plunge away into the wilderness. She was like a brutally-treated horse. She'd have to set her own pace.

By the time Kareena wandered off for the third time it

was midafternoon. The wind was still rising, the waves were breaking hard on the beach, and the sky was turning gray. Blade hoped Kareena would come back soon and not let herself be caught outside the shelter of the Hovercraft by the storm.

By the time she'd been gone half an hour, Blade was pacing up and down outside the Hovercraft like a caged lion. He had to wonder if she might have finally run off. If so, the coming storm would make it almost impossible for him to pick up her trail.

Blade paced for a few minutes longer, then decided to throw caution to the rising winds. He hadn't brought Kareena this far simply to let her die in the wilderness. He went back inside the Hovercraft, and when he came out he was carrying a laser rifle and his jacket pockets were full of hand grenades.

Although Kareena hadn't left much of a trail he could follow, Blade knew which way she'd gone. He tramped up the hill, rifle in hand and eyes searching the landscape ahead. By the time the Hovercraft was out of sight behind him, the day had faded to a weird half-twilight and the wind was turning cold.

A mile inland he came over the crest of a low ridge and found himself looking down into a narrow valley where a few stunted trees grew among the rocks. Kareena was tied to one of those trees, her face pale and blood running down her chin. Seven men in ragged outfits of leather and fur were standing around her or sitting by a small fire. All of them had swords or spears, and one of them had a battered laser rifle as well.

Blade felt like raising his own rifle and blasting away but knew the men down there could easily kill Kareena before they went down themselves. He'd try diplomacy first, rather than brute force. The fact that Kareena was still clothed and apparently not badly hurt suggested that those Tribesmen might listen to argument.

Blade slung his rifle aside, but unbuttoned the flaps over the pockets where he carried the grenades. They would be his ace in the hole, if he could use them without hurting Kareena. Then he stood up, his empty hands held in clear sight. The Tribesmen shouted and pointed, then the largest of them stepped away from the fire, repeating Blade's gesture. So far so good. Blade started down into the valley.

The exchange of peace gestures was the last bit of clear communication for several minutes. It wasn't that Blade didn't understand the language of the Tribesmen. It was a recognizable dialect of the universal language of the Land. The problem was that they hardly used the language to communicate, preferring an elaborate code of grunts, gestures, and headshakes which they seemed to expect Blade to understand. Perhaps the Doimari or other city traders did, but as far as he was concerned the Tribesmen might have been speaking some South American Indian language he'd never even heard of, let alone learned! The computer's work on his brain was no help at all.

After a while the leader seemed to understand that what they had here was a failure to communicate. He waved his followers back and stepped close to Blade. Blade felt like gagging at the chief's smell.

"Your woman?" he said, pointing at Kareena.

"My woman."

"You are in land of Hoirccchhh." Or at least the name of the tribe sounded like that to Blade.

"I have heard of the Hoirccchhh," said Blade, hoping he'd pronounced it right. "They are a strong and brave people."

The chief smiled. "Yes. Strong and brave. We take a price to come on our land. You pay with this woman for us, for tonight."

Blade saw Kareena stiffen and had to fight not to do so himself. The chief was asking for the right to gang-rape Kareena as the price of peace between him and Blade. Blade wondered if he hadn't wasted everybody's time trying to be diplomatic.

"My woman is not strong," he said in a level voice.

"Then why you keep her?" said the chief. "You are strong warrior, need strong woman to give you sons."

"She is strong enough for me," said Blade. He noticed that the seven men were now forming a circle around him. The man with the laser rifle was in plain sight, though. Also, the men were now all out of easy reach of Kareena.

144

"She strong enough for you, strong enough for us," said the chief bluntly. "You pay for coming on our land with her, or some other way."

Blade was tempted to play for time by seeming to agree, then Kareena raised her head. The trapped look in her eyes drove the temptation out of Blade. He wasn't going to add *anything* to Kareena's burden, even if it meant greater danger for him.

Unfortunately the chief seemed to take Blade's look as a sign of agreement. One of his men stepped toward Kareena, gripped her jacket with both hands, and tore it down to her waist. She hissed like a snake and closed her eyes. Then the man reached inside her shirt and started to fondle her breast, and she screamed.

Blade had never heard a scream like that from a living throat. He hoped he would never hear one like it again. His hand dropped toward the grenade pocket. Even without pulling the pin, he could throw one like a stone and take out the rifleman.

Then Kareena screamed again, and Blade stopped thinking of grenades or any other modern weapons. He wanted *blood*, preferably shed with his own hands. His control snapped completely but his skills didn't desert him. In the next minute the Tribesmen paid a grisly price for all that Blade and Kareena had endured in Doimar.

Blade leaped completely over the campfire to close with the rifleman. He tore the weapon out of the man's hands and drove the butt into his face so hard it not only crushed his nose but also blinded him. The rifle broke in two under the impact but Blade hung on to the barrel and used it as a short spear. A swordsman screamed as the jagged end of the barrel destroyed his manhood, then fell over backward into the fire and screamed again. A man coming at Blade with a spear tripped over the fallen man and went down almost at Blade's feet. Blade jumped on his back and stamped down with both feet, cracking the spine like a twig. Then he drew his own sword and engaged two men at once.

That took him only a little longer. He slashed through a spear and one of the arms holding it. Then he closed with

145

the man, grabbed him, and spun him around so that he took in his own stomach a sword thrust his comrade had meant for Blade.

Finally Blade dropped the dying man and broke the swordsman's neck with a karate blow. Five down, two to go.

The other two weren't standing to fight. They were running toward the crest of the hill, to get away or perhaps bring reinforcements. Blade snatched a grenade from his pocket, pulled the pin, and threw. The grenade exploded just as it hit one man in the back of the neck, and his head and shoulders vanished in a bloody spray. Fragments and concussion knocked the last man off his feet. He was still struggling to rise when Blade caught up with him and pounded his head against the rocks until he lay still.

When Blade came back down the hill, he found that Kareena had fainted. He cut her loose with his sword, and was lifting her in his arms when a bolt of lightning hit the crest of the hill. The light half-dazzled him, the thunder left his ears ringing, and sulphur stank in his nostrils. Then the rain poured down, washing away the sulphur smell but soaking them both to the skin in moments.

The journey back to the Hovercraft was a nightmare in the storm. Fear that other Tribesmen might have found it didn't ease Blade's mind. But it was intact and unharmed when they reached it, although the rising wind was shaking it. He didn't dare try moving to another place in this storm—they'd be blown out onto the lake the moment they lifted clear of the ground.

Instead he turned the cabin heat up as high as it would go, then stripped off Kareena's clothes and wrapped her in everything dry he could find. She woke up while he was heating some soup.

"Blade, are we—where are we?"

"In the Oltec machine, on the shore of Lake Mison, a long way from Doimar. Right where we were a few hours ago."

"Then—it was a dream, those Tribesmen and—your fight?"

"It wasn't a dream, Kareena. They'd captured you. I fought them and killed them."

146

"Yes. I remember now. But—Blade, you didn't need to fight. They weren't going to kill you. They were only—only . . ." She shuddered.

Blade desperately wanted to hold her but restrained himself. "Yes. I would not allow that. I wouldn't have allowed anything that happened in Doimar, if there'd been any other way to learn the city's secrets. I had no choice. Believe me, I had none."

"Blade—you really—didn't—betray Kaldak?" Her words were getting slurred.

"No. They haven't learned anything about us, and we've learned everything about them. Not only that, but everything about where Kaldak's Oltec can be found. Kareena, you went through hell, but now we can fight Doimar and *win!*"

"Fight," she said. "Fight—like you fought for—me." Her hand crept out from under the blankets and reached for Blade's. Before their fingers touched her eyes drifted shut, and she was asleep. She was also smiling.

Blade sat there, looking at the smile. He supposed he ought to feel dirty, even animallike. He'd certainly slaughtered those seven Tribesmen more like an animal than like a man. Yet he could hardly feel that gang of would-be rapists was much of a loss to any Dimension, and Kareena's smile was worth a lot.

Chapter 20

Kareena was still smiling when she woke up after the storm. In the evening twilight Blade moved the Hovercraft a few miles down the shore, out of reach of anyone searching for the missing Tribesmen. Then he and Kareena both got their first really good night's sleep since leaving Kaldak on the way to Gilmarg.

The next morning they left the shore of Lake Mison and headed out across the plains. Blade took his time, now that they were beyond the reach of both the Doimari and the Tribes. They were more than halfway home, but it would still be a long walk for Blade and probably an impossible one for Kareena.

After some arguing, Kareena took off her trousers and let Blade examine her injured leg. As he'd suspected, the fracture was setting slightly crooked. In Home Dimension it would have been a simple matter to rebreak the leg and set it properly. In this Dimension there'd be no point in putting Kareena through another painful ordeal with not much chance of success. So she would always have a slight limp as a souvenir of her captivity in Doimar.

She shrugged when Blade gave her the bad news. "I'm still too happy just to be alive to worry about being crippled. Perhaps in time we'll find Oltec which can finish healing the leg. Meanwhile, we've already found Oltec which will let me fight the Doimari sitting down."

It took them several days to cross the plains and reach the hills which marked the boundary of the lands claimed by Kaldak. Blade stopped once to shoot and butcher a wild munfan, to give them a change from the wholesome but dull emergency rations in the Hovercraft. That night they had a feast of munfan steaks broiled over a brushwood fire. Kareena sat across the fire from Blade, eating with the first real appetite he'd seen her show, happily smearing her face and her bare arms with grease. She looked like the warrior-queen she'd been when Blade first saw her.

By the time they reached the hills, Kareena was willing to be naked in front of Blade and have him naked in front of her. She still didn't care to have him touch her, but she was willing to touch him. Her fingers hadn't lost their skill in massaging kinks out of muscles, and after hours hunched over the controls Blade welcomed those massages.

They met a Kaldakan patrol the morning after they crossed the hills and nearly fought a battle with it. The Hovercraft had Doimar's insignia on the hull, which confused the Kaldakans. The Kaladkans were entirely armed

148

and equipped with Oltec, which confused Blade. Fortunately someone in the patrol knew Blade, and several knew
Kareena, so the confusion was settled before any shots
were fired.

Blade climbed down from the Hovercraft, and the Kaldakans gathered around him while he told his story briefly.
At the same time he was studying them. Now close up, he
could easily tell they were not Doimari. Their Oltec was all
new and shiny, and they didn't wear it as though they were
used to it. Two of them were wearing hand grenades hung
by the rings. Blade quickly corrected that.

"The Lords of the Law must watch over fools, or both of
you would be dead by now," he said sharply. He showed
them the correct way of handling grenades, then asked,
"Why are you all armed with Oltec? Has there been a new
find? Or did Peython give everything there was to the
guards on the border?"

"Oh, Peython gave first choice to us of the border, sure
enough," said the leader. "But no one in Kaldak is short of
Oltec now. When Bairam and Saorm came back from Gilmarg, they turned out every man and woman as you urged.
We tore the city apart almost stone by stone. There is Oltec
now for many more things than killing Doimari, although
we will have to do that—"

Laughter interrupted the man and made Blade turn
around. Kareena was standing in the Hovercraft's hatch,
laughing wildly. For a moment Blade was frightened,
thinking she'd gone into hysterics. Then he realized that
she was just amused. He had a nasty feeling he knew what
was making her laugh.

"All right, Kareena," he said when she'd quieted down.
"What's the joke?"

"I'm sorry, Blade. But when he was telling you they'd
found all the Oltec themselves, you looked like this." She
opened her mouth in an idiotic gape with her tongue sticking out and rolled her eyes up in her head.

"Did I really—?" Blade began to ask the men around
him, then shook his head. "No, don't tell me."

It was embarrassing to work hard at the risk of your life
for weeks on end, then come home and find somebody else
had done most of the same job while you were away. But it

was also good news. The Kaldakans' work would save months in arming and equipping their army with Oltec, and might very well save their city.

Also, if Kareena could laugh this way after learning that her ordeal might have been unnecessary, she was on her way to being healed. Every war has its inevitable victims, but it was good to think Kareena wouldn't be a victim of this one.

It was normally five days' travel from where Blade met the patrol to Kaldak. In the Hovercraft Blade covered the distance in less than five hours. They arrived in plenty of time for Peython to put on a truly magnificent party that evening, celebrating his daughter's safe return and Blade's discovery of Doimar's secrets.

Blade learned that in his absence, the Lawmakers had already met to begin a reappraisal of the existing Law. So many changes had occurred in Kaldak after the discovery of the hoards of Oltec that the Law had to be carefully rewritten. What was more, it was decided that Blade was a great hero and that there would be no need for a meeting of the Gathering to pass judgment on him.

Blade also had time to learn exactly what else the Kaldakans did in his absence. It was really quite a lot, even if most of it was done by trial and error. The only person who really seemed to have known what he was doing was the merchant Saorm.

"Did you know more about the cellars of Kaldak?" said Blade. "Or did being the father of Bairam's future bride inspire you again?"

"A family can always use more honor fairly gained," said Saorm. He grinned. "As for the other question—does it matter now?"

It was on the tip of Blade's tongue to tell Saorm that if he'd spoken out earlier and admitted to his knowledge of Kaldak's store of Oltec, he might have saved his chief's daughter a gruesome ordeal. He decided to hold his peace. No one in Kaldak except her father and Bairam knew the details of Kareena's captivity, and Blade wanted to keep it that way. Also, Saorm had done his best according to his own standards. That "best" had not been really too bad, either in Gilmarg or here in Kaldak.

The Kaldakans found many things they knew how to use, and more things they thought they knew how to use, such as the hand grenades. There'd been several fatal accidents, and plenty of croakers to proclaim that this was what came of meddling with the Law. When Blade studied what the Kaldakans were doing with machinery and weapons they barely understood, he was surprised they hadn't wiped out a good part of their city.

They'd even discovered the waldoes and their command center. Fortunately Peython and Sidas prevented any dangerous experiments here. "Other Oltec weapons kill only those close to them if they go wrong," said Sidas. "These steel men could walk through Kaldak, killing everyone they found. They could do us more harm than the Doimari!"

At the party Blade drank a toast to Peython, Sidas, and their common sense. In fact he drank quite a number of toasts, but still managed to get to bed early. There was more work facing him than he liked to think about. He suspected that he'd be up at dawn tomorrow, and for many days after that.

Blade was right.

Part of his work was minor details, like teaching the Kaldakans *not* to hang grenades by their rings. Most of this detail he quickly delegated to Bairam, Sidas, or Kareena. With the help of a cane Kareena got around well enough, and keeping busy kept her mind off her memories of Doimar.

Another part of Blade's work was training Kaldak's infantry. They would need new tactics, now that they were heavily equipped with Oltec themselves and facing an enemy even better equipped. They had to be taught how to concentrate the fire of their own rifles, scatter to avoid the Doimaran mortars, and take cover to avoid the lasers of the waldoes. With Peython's help Blade picked fifty of the brightest leaders of the Kaldakan infantry and put them through a week-long crash course in tactics. During that week Blade got hardly any sleep at all.

151

The results he got would still have made a Home Dimension company commander have a stroke. The Kaldakans' casualties were going to be appalling. However, they were tough, enthusiastic, and knew they were going to be fighting for their lives and the future of their city. They might just be able to take those casualties and go on fighting. Blade hoped so. There wasn't much else he could hope to do with the Kaldakan infantry in the time available.

Blade had better luck with the waldoes. The first thing he did was find out how many of Kaldak's waldoes and control chairs were still working. That meant another week of getting to bed at midnight and getting up at dawn. Fortunately he was able to teach a few Kaldakans how to make the tests, although in a "monkey see, monkey do" fashion. With their help he soon knew there were about a hundred working waldoes and at least fifty control chairs which might last out a battle.

Using the waldoes was not hard to learn. It wasn't so easy that Blade could hope to teach it to fifty Kaldakans in the few weeks or at most months he had left. Even if the Doimari didn't attack by then, he himself would probably be snatched back to Home Dimension.

Not for the first time, Blade wished he had some control over the time of his return to Home Dimension. Lord Leighton would howl at the idea, since he didn't like the idea of guinea pigs with a will of their own. Even J might have doubts, fearing Blade would run unnecessary risks to finish some minor task.

Blade wouldn't admit either point. He was a man, not a guinea pig, and he trusted his own judgment of how many risks he should run. He absolutely did not like the idea of being completely at somebody's whim when he had important work to do. So far unexpected returns from Dimension X hadn't done worse than embarrass him. A few times they'd actually saved his life. Sooner or later things would work out differently. He'd be snatched home with something vital left undone. If he had to go home now before he'd taught Kaldak how to use the waldoes, the city might still go down in defeat. At best thousands of people would die who might have otherwise lived.

Unfortunately Blade was nearly helpless. Lord Leighton

and J were both in Home Dimension, and they'd probably turn a deaf ear to his arguments even after he got home. All he could do now was make sure that he left behind enough knowledge of the waldoes to give the Kaldakans a fighting chance.

Blade explained his plan to Peython over a dinner of roast fish and plenty of beer.

"I'll set all of the waldoes and all of the chairs on a single group of frequencies—" he began.

"A single what?" asked the chief.

Blade stopped to quickly explain radio. Peython took in the explanation with only a few questions. "So any chair can send the Voice to any waldo," he said. "And any waldo can send back what it hears and sees to the man in any chair?"

"Yes. A man can climb into any of the chairs and control any or all of the waldoes, without having to waste time finding the correct frequency. This way all of the waldoes can be controlled by one man if necessary. He will have to make all of them do the same thing, of course—"

"That is much better than having none of them do anything," said Peython.

"Very true. In fact, I plan to have only three or four other people in control chairs at the same time, each controlling waldoes of their own."

"No more?"

"I can teach only three or four people how to fight and also how to teach others. Kaldak will be better off with three or four people who know everything than with thirty or forty who know only a little." Peython nodded.

When the Doimari advanced, Blade and his trained operators would march Kaldak's waldoes out to a hiding place close to the chosen battlefield. That would have to be within fifty miles of Kaldak, because there was no hope of getting any sort of radio relay.

"What if the Doimari have such a 'relay,' as you call it?"

Blade knew the Doimari probably did have the relay system now, thanks to his discovery of the Hovercraft, but that couldn't be helped. "As fast as possible we attack the machine carrying the Voice and destroy it."

"And if the Doimari do not march until they have many

Voice relays?" said Peython. From someone other than Peython this persistent question might have annoyed Blade. As it was, it implied that Peython wanted to learn for himself most of what Blade wanted to teach. So Blade didn't mind explaining anything Peython wanted explained.

"That will take until next year. I do not think they will wait that long. If they do not know of our new Oltec, they will think we are still weak and helpless. If they do know of it, they will also know they must strike soon, before we can learn to use what we have discovered. They have nothing at all to gain by waiting. Also, I think the quarrel between the Seekers and the infantry will keep them from stopping to think clearly about almost anything."

"I hope we will not have such a quarrel between those who love Oltec and those who love the Law in Kaldak," said Peython. He poured himself more beer and grinned. "However, I have thought of ways to make sure that those who love the Law can do no harm to us in the war. After that, we shall see." He drank, then poured some more beer for Blade.

Blade drank more than he'd planned that night, so when he left Peython he also was not thinking too clearly about anything. He drifted back to his quarters without really being aware of covering the distance.

He now had four rooms of his own. That was more than he needed, but Peython refused to listen to Blade's protests. "Nobody was turned out into the streets to make room for you," the chief said. "And I will not give you less than you got from Feragga of Doimar! So for once in your life, Blade, you will do as I tell you!"

"Yes, Peython," said Blade with a wry grin.

Blade's new bedroom was the farthest room from the main door. Blade left clothes and weapons in each of the first three rooms, until he was naked when he entered the bedroom. Then he stopped abruptly, a few steps short of climbing into bed. The room was dark, but he saw a long bulge in the furs and a few trailing curls of dark hair on the pillow.

Instantly Blade's thoughts were clear, even though he wasn't exactly sober. He wasn't worried about an assassin. If there was going to be an attack, it would have come

154

already. What he suspected was waiting for him in the bed might be more difficult to handle. He bent over the bed, rested a hand on the curls of hair, and murmured softly to the bulge in the furs, "Hello, Kareena."

The furs churned briefly, then Kareena's head popped out. She was smiling. "You would have been embarrassed if it had been Geyrna or some other woman."

"I didn't think it was." Blade sat down on the bed and took the hand Kareena stretched out to him. Then he bent over and kissed her upturned lips. They were rigid and cold under his for a moment. Then they trembled and broke apart. When he thrust his tongue slowly into her mouth, he felt her body stiffen. He didn't draw back, and after another moment some of the tension went out of her. Her own tongue crept up to meet his.

That saved a good many words. He now knew what she wanted—a night with him which would finish healing the wounds from Doimar. He didn't know whether he or any other man could give it. Well, in love as in war, a man could only do the best job he could do in the time available.

Without lifting his mouth from Kareena's, Blade slid one hand under the furs and down her body. Three fingers slid down the cleft between her breasts, while two others played with a nipple. Once more the response took a little while, but when it came it was gratifying. The nipple hardened, and Kareena gave a soft little whimper.

An inch at a time, Blade worked one hand down Kareena's body while he went on kissing her. After a while he had to lift his lips from hers, but by then her eyes were closed and she was breathing hard. Now he had two hands and his lips free, and he used all of them everywhere they could go.

He'd taken less time and trouble with women he knew to be virgins than he took with Kareena. He held himself back as if on a steel chain, although before long Kareena was not only obviously aroused but was trying to arouse him. The furs were thrown off, they lay beside each other on the bed, and Kareena's long-fingered hands were roaming up and down Blade's body with a life of their own.

Blade stopped worrying about Kareena's response now, but still held back from entering her. He wanted it to be

155

absolutely *right* for her. Anything less would be hardly more than another rape, as far as he was concerned. He only hoped he could ignore the growing fire in his own body long enough.

Then Kareena's breath rattled in her throat, and Blade could make out distorted, half-coherent words. "Blade— please—now—before—" Her voice failed her, and she could only gasp. Smoothly Blade shifted position and, with all the care and self-restraint he had left, entered her.

She went rigid under him for long enough to make him wonder if he'd made a horrible mistake. Then her arms went around him, her thighs clamped hard on his hips, and her lips came up to nuzzle his neck. Blade immediately stopped worrying, and before much longer he stopped thinking at all. The world shrank down to Kareena's body under him, her skin and her breasts and the warmth which held him so closely, and finally her happy cry of release.

That was the first night. The second night was better, the third better still, and the fourth as good as any man and woman could wish. After that Kareena came regularly, and within a month Blade had given Kareena the same gift he'd given the seven women of Doimar. She was pregnant.

She wasn't sure whether to curse him or bless him. A child of her own was the dream of any woman of the Land. On the other hand—

"If this keeps me out of the war with Doimar, I'll never forgive you!" she said.

"Don't worry, daughter," said Peython. "If I know Feragga of Doimar, she'll attack long before the child has grown enough to slow you." His eyes met Blade's, and they shared an unspoken thought: *If only we could keep Kareena out of the battle completely.* However, they both knew her too well.

"I hope so," said Kareena. "I owe the Doimari a debt, and the sooner it's paid the better."

Peython was an accurate prophet. The morning after the party to celebrate Kareena's pregnancy, word came from the frontier patrols. The army of Doimar was on the march.

Chapter 21

Nungor was already half-dressed when Feragga got out of bed. When she was barefoot and he wore boots, the top of his head almost reached her shoulder. She bent down to kiss him, rumpled his hair, then started pulling on her clothes. Through the door of the tent trickled the dawn light and the sounds of the Doimari camp coming awake.

Nungor heard the crackle of wood fires, the bubbling of stewpots, the curses of munfan drivers, and the growls and hisses of the munfans themselves. Sometimes he heard the crack of whips as Kaldakan prisoners were driven to their day's work. Once he even heard the whir and whine as the Seekers tested their new Oltec machine.

Nungor didn't quite know what to think about that machine. On the one hand, without the machine and the Voice equipment it carried, the hundred Fighting Machines the army had with it would not be so strong: This far from home, the Voices from Doimar could hardly get the Fighting Machines to walk straight most of the time, let alone fight well. But on the other hand, Nungor and his infantry had no control over the Carrying Machines, which were claimed by the Seekers. That made the whole affair of the machines eat at Nungor's guts like a meal of rotten meat. But Feragga had said it must be so, and then the best man at handling the machine turned out to be a Seeker! There wasn't much Nungor could do about Feragga even if he wanted to, but he could do something about that cursed Seeker! The man wasn't going to survive more than a single day beyond the last battle of the war, if Nungor had to kill him with his own hands!

Now another question nagged at Nungor. As the Doimari penetrated the frontier of Kaldak, there were few Kaldakans to be seen, let alone taken prisoner. Had Blade returned to Kaldak and told the people to retreat so far, instead of giving battle on the frontiers where the Fighting Machines would be deadly? Maybe he had. Even so, Blade had already lost all chance of victory before leaving Doimar, by showing how the Carrying Machines could be used.

"Think we'll meet them today?" said Feragga's voice behind him. He turned. She was ready for battle, complete with body armor. Since there was no one single set of armor large enough to fit her, she wore two fastened together. Nungor hoped this improvisation would protect her. The thought of losing her to the Kaldakans hurt, though not as much as it would have hurt to lose her to that cursed Blade!

"They have to turn and fight sometime," said Nungor. "We've chased them three days' march across their own land and burned many of their farms. We're only two days from Kaldak itself. Peython's gambling with his people's loyalty. Or do you suppose this is Blade's doing?"

Feragga shrugged. "Don't underestimate Peython. He's the sort of man to come up with new answers when he faces new problems. I suspect we'll have to beat him not just once but several times before he gives up. Fortunately there won't be many more chiefs like him, so once we've got Kaldak we've got half the Land."

"Pray that it be so," said Nungor evenly. He was getting a little tired of Feragga's evading a discussion of Blade. He could understand why she was embarrassed at the treachery of a man she'd so nearly taken to her bed, even at the cost of her long comradeship with the War Captain. What bothered him more was not knowing if her spy network in Kaldak had broken down. If it had, they couldn't know if the Kaldakans were planning any surprises, and it was going to be hard for him to plan more than the simplest battle.

Very well, he would plan a simple battle. He'd keep all the foot fighters together, and the first time the Kaldakans showed themselves he'd hit them with everything he had except the Fighting Machines. The machines would guard the rear while the footmen stamped the Kaldakans into the ground. That would start off the war with a good solid victory and maybe frighten the Kaldakans out of pulling any surprises, Blade or no Blade!

He squeezed Feragga's hand and side by side they went out into the morning to take their place among their soldiers.

The Hovercraft whined through the nearly deserted streets of Kaldak toward the entrance to the waldoes' command center. Kareena was at the controls, with Blade in the other chair and six armed infantrymen behind them in the cabin. Blade and Kareena hadn't spent all their time together in the past month making love. In good weather she could now handle the Hovercraft almost as well as Blade.

Blade looked up at the blue sky. It was a fine autumn day, and gave every sign of staying that way. That was good news. Rain or mist might not hide Blade's surprises from the Doimar, and would certainly make it harder for Peython to command Kaldak's army.

The Hovercraft stopped at a barricade of piled rubble, logs, furniture, and steel beams. The men at the barricade pushed away stones at one end, then Kareena steered the Hovercraft through the gap without hitting the wall more than twice. Building and manning the street barricades was one job given to the Kaldakans who refused to fight with all the new Oltec. Another job was carrying food, beer, munfan fodder, medicines, and other Lawful supplies to the army outside Kaldak.

A few die-hards refused to do anything at all. They said Kaldak was now so far outside the Law that it was morally unfit to survive. "We would rather die than befoul ourselves this way!" they cried. "Very well," replied Peython. "You shall have your wish." After the first twenty executions, the rest of the die-hards got the message.

The barricades would probably turn out to be an unnecessary precaution, since the Doimari probably wouldn't get to Kaldak in force until the main Kaldakan army was destroyed. Then the barricades would be useless and the barricade defenders could take to their heels with a clear conscience. Patrols or a few stray waldoes might still slip away from the battlefield and reach the city. Making it hard for these to move freely and giving cover to the men fighting them would save lives. Blade knew this fight was going to be a bloody shambles no matter who won, but he wasn't going to throw lives away.

When they drove up to the entrance to the underground command center, Sidas was standing by the door, wearing only boots and a loincloth. He greeted Blade and Kareena, then winked at them and ordered the six soldiers out of the Hovercraft, to give them privacy for their farewell.

I am not in love with Kareena, Blade told himself for the hundredth time. He even believed it for the hundredth time. That didn't make it any easier to see her heading off to the battle while he sat safe in a hole in the ground. When her lips were on his and she was obviously trying not to cry, it was even harder than usual.

"Take care of yourself, Kareena," he said finally. "If you don't, your father surely will."

She snorted. "He'll be too busy fighting the battle to worry about me."

"Don't bet on it," he said, stroking her hair. "Or you may find you're not too old for a spanking."

"Yes, Blade," she said with mock humility. Then she kissed him again and signaled to the infantry guards to come back. Blade climbed out and watched while she started the Hovercraft again.

He kept watching until it was out of sight around the corner, on its way back to where Peython and the army of Kaldak waited for the battle. He knew she would probably be safe, whether she wanted to be or not. She was acting as both chief of staff and chauffeur to her father, and in the normal course of things she'd be nowhere near the front lines. However, the "normal course of things" in any battle could suddenly change, and in this battle more easily than most. Which reminded Blade—

"How are our Scouts doing?"

Sidas clenched both fists and punched them together. It was the Kaldakan equivalent of crossing your fingers.

"They haven't failed us yet," he added, with a grin.

160

"Good." The scouting system was one of Blade's inventions. He suspected it would give the Kaldakans an advantage not because it worked so well, but because it was the only thing of its kind in this whole Dimension. At least it was simple enough so that it *might* work. Several waldoes not fit for combat had been walked to points overlooking possible battle sites. Then their audio and visual pickups were activated and left on. A man in a control chair could watch the countryside simply by switching from one waldo to another. Human scouts filled in the gaps between the waldoes. If they saw something, they would send a messenger to the nearest waldo and have it pass the word.

Once word came to the command center, the problem was getting it back to the Kaldakan army. For that the human scouts had smoke signals and messenger birds. Some of the scout waldoes could fire their lasers in a coded pattern. Blade could even make a waldo write messages in the dirt, if everything else failed, as it probably would—

Blade realized that Sidas was trying to get his attention. "Word from below, Blade. The Doimari are still coming on, all bunched up together."

"Good." Either Nungor was underestimating his opponents or he had some plan of his own which meant keeping his army massed. Blade thought the second was more likely, but either way it played into his hands for now. Once battle was joined things might change, though. They might not change too fast for him, but they would probably change too fast for the improvised Kaldakan army. They were long on courage, but still rather short on training.

"Who's in the chair now?" asked Blade.

"Bairam."

"How is he?"

Sidas shrugged eloquently. He was not going to say anything out loud against his chief's son, but, on the other hand, he wasn't going to hide important truths from Blade. So Bairam was still too excitable for safety. That at least was no surprise. "Let's go down. I'd better take over. We may have to get the waldoes moving fast."

The Carrying Machine was moving so slowly that Rehna climbed out of the top hatch and sat with her legs dangling down inside. She still moved carefully. She could not be sure yet, but she thought she might be carrying Blade's child. If that was so, she hoped that the coming battle would be the last against Kaldak as well as the first. She wanted to be among the Seekers who proved in battle the value of their work. She also wanted to bear that child, even if it came from the seed of a man who'd betrayed Doimar. A man's seed did not bind his child.

An explosion behind her made her turn around. Smoke rose from the crest of the hill at the mouth of the valley. They must have blown up the Fighting Machine the Kaldakans abandoned there. It always hurt her to see Oltec destroyed, particularly the Fighting Machines, which were the masterpieces of the Tower Builders. However, the Kaldakans had ruined the machine so completely there was nothing else to do with it. They couldn't have got much use out of it, either.

Rehna looked ahead again. The valley was broad enough so that Doimar's army was advancing in three columns. The one on the right moved along the valley floor, closest to the steep, wooded hills on the north side. In the middle moved the Fighting Machines, with the Carrying Machine in the middle of them. Most of the hundred Fighting Machines which started from Doimar were still marching as if they could go on to the end of the Land. Rehna hoped they would, even if she wasn't there to see them. The left-hand column followed the crest of the grassy ridge on the south side of the valley.

The Carrying Machine swung to the right so violently that Rehna nearly lost her balance. As it swung back, it narrowly missed one of the Fighting Machines. Through the open hatch Rehna heard curses. The less experienced of the two drivers was at the controls. He was only good enough for level ground, and the valley floor seemed to be getting rougher the farther they went.

Rehna leaned down through the hatch and shouted, "Get clear of the Fighting Machines and stop. Sutro, you'd better take over."

"Ah, Rehna, he's half-asleep. He can't—"

"Yes, I can. Sorry about this, but Rehna's right. I'd better get us through the valley."

The second driver cursed again, but obeyed. The machine settled to the ground, and silence fell so suddenly that it was almost frightening. It was only when the Carrying Machine stopped that you realized how noisy it was.

Then the silence was broken by another explosion. Rehna looked back, saw the smoke there was long gone, heard still another explosion, and realized it came from ahead. When she looked toward the north side of the valley, she saw the little puffs of smoke from hand-thrown fire bombs. Here and there through the smoke fire-beams flickered green, going both uphill and down.

"Sutro, quick! Get us to the hill over there!" She waved frantically to the south. "The Kaldakans are attacking. We have to be where we can carry the Voice. Hurry!"

Then she slid down inside the cabin and pulled the hatch shut behind her. Her mouth was dry, and her stomach was so twisted that she was afraid of vomiting. She couldn't do that, not today, when the Seekers were about to prove beyond any doubt that *they* held the future of Doimar and its Empire in their hands—or rather, the hands of the Fighting Machines marching around her.

Chapter 22

Nungor and Feragga ran up to the Carrying Machine. As usual Nungor had to take two steps to her one to keep up with her. He'd long since stopped worrying about the kind of spectacle he made doing that. He would not let Feragga go alone into this battle if he could help it.

With a boost from Feragga, Nungor scrambled up on the roof of the machine. Wires snagged his feet and he hoped none of them were carrying the Voice. A living wire doing that could kill.

"Get your Fighting Machines back up here!" he shouted down into the hatch. "The enemy is in the trees, if they're anywhere, and the machines can't go in there."

"They could go up the valley, then get around behind—" began Rehna.

"They won't go out of our sight!" snapped Nungor. "And neither will you. You people stay right here and carry the Voice to the Fighting Machines until I tell you to stop." He caught himself short of adding the ridiculous threat, "Or I'll have your Carrying Machine destroyed." That might lose the battle and it would certainly mean open war between the Seekers and the foot soldiers.

"We shall obey, Nungor," Rehna replied coldly. "But let Feragga give us the same order."

After Nungor explained the situation, Feragga did so. "This is not the time or place for the Fighting Machines," she said. "They can hardly see the enemy, let alone strike him. When we know where the rest of the Kaldakans are, *then* perhaps we can send the Fighting Machines to attack on their own."

"Do you swear this, Feragga?"

"No, I don't and I won't. The battle has just started. Now forget your Seekers' pride and obey, curse you!"

"Yes, Feragga." Rehna sounded sullen.

When Feragga climbed down she found Nungor checking his equipment. "I'm going down there and lead the attack. This is the first battle against Kaldak, and I'm not going to let anyone else do the work."

"Including me?"

"Feragga, I didn't mean—"

"Probably you didn't. Anyway, one of us had better stay with the Fighting Machines and keep watch on the Seekers. I'll do that better than you, and you won't be worrying about me."

"Feragga, I—"

She bent over and kissed him. "Go with your fortune, Nungor."

As Nungor ran down the hill, he noticed that much of the work of preparing the attack was already done. The riflemen were already spreading out, giving the enemy a harder target. In the bottom of the valley, the fire-bomb throwers were in place. They would do more to chase the Kaldakans out of the trees than all those damned Fighting Machines! A fire-beam could not jump over the top of a tree and kill a man behind it!

Kareena's leg was hurting as she made her way forward through the trees. Fortunately it wasn't hurting so bad that she had to use her rifle as a cane. She wanted to use the rifle to kill a few more Doimari before her father discovered that she was missing.

From the noise coming through the trees, it would be a while before anyone noticed anything not directly in front of their noses. There were more explosions from the—what did Blade call them?—'mortars'?—then rifle fire. The Doimari must be trying to kill as many Kaldakans as they could with the mortars before sending their foot soldiers up the hill again. That made sense. Without the mortars the thousand Kaldakans hiding in the trees could probably stay there all day, killing twice their own number of Doimari.

A mortar bomb exploded in the trees overhead, showering splinters of wood and hot metal around Kareena. Two more explosions left someone in the distance screaming in agony. Kareena set her jaw against the sound. However many Kaldakans died here today, it would be fewer than would have died without Blade and his knowledge.

Off to the left a whole company of somebody's soldiers seemed to be firing lasers. She listened but didn't hear the heavier sound of the lasers from the Doimari waldoes. She did hear an ugly crackling of flames and smelled wood smoke.

Wham, bam, crash! It seemed that the sky was falling on the forest and the forest was falling on her. She dove to the ground behind a fallen trunk as branches and hot metal rained down on her again. Something jabbed the back of her good leg like a wasp with a red-hot stinger. She ignored it when she discovered that she was sharing the trunk with someone else, someone she recognized.

"Saorm!"

"Kareena! What are you doing here?"

"I might ask the same question."

"I asked—" Mortar shells interrupted them, and the smell of smoke grew stronger. They heard someone screaming for help to be moved before the fire got to her.

"I asked first," Saorm finished.

"The Hovercraft ran out of power cells of the right size. I came up to see how the fighting was going."

"Your machine should be moving again fairly soon. I came up with supplies. We brought fire—I mean, power cells, of every size." He rose and cupped a hand to one ear. "I'm going to pull that woman clear of the fire, then go back."

"Saorm, don't—!" The howl of falling mortar bombs interrupted her. She buried her head in her arms and screamed as explosions crashed all around them. She didn't feel anything herself this time, but she heard someone close by cry out.

When she raised her head again, she saw who it was. Saorm lay slumped over the fallen trunk, blood spurting from the stump of one leg. Kareena pulled off her scarf and started binding it around the stump. Sarom shook his head and opened his mouth. Little bubbles of blood came out, and also hoarse words.

"Don't—bother. Hit in the belly—you tie it up, I die slow. Just—make sure—Geyrna gets what's hers."

"I swear it, Saorm."

"Good. Wanted to see—her children, but—what a man wants and what—the Law gives—aren't always the same."

He couldn't speak after that, but Kareena held his hand until his eyes closed. By then the smoke was so thick Kareena was half-choking, and in the murk she could make out Kaldakan soldiers coming toward her. Some were half-naked, their clothes burned off, others limping or with one arm dangling useless. Some who were crippled or blinded were being led or carried along. They were all bringing out their weapons, and those who weren't in too much pain to talk called out greetings to Kareena.

She wanted to weep, partly from the smoke but more from pride in the way Kaldak's people were standing up to the battle. The soldiers of Blade's own England couldn't have done better, she thought.

It was time to join the retreating soldiers. There was nothing more she could do here, and she might be needed at the controls of the Hovercraft. The battle was getting to the point where her father might need to change his orders suddenly, and that could mean moving.

One more thing to do, though—make sure Saorm's body wasn't left for the flames. She called four unwounded men over, they lifted it, then followed her out of the smoke toward the waiting army of Kaldak.

Through the eyes of the last of the scout waldoes, Blade saw the Kaldakan advance guard streaming out of the burning forest. Good. They were retreating fast, but they weren't routed, even though that forest fire was something he hadn't expected. Anyway, it would be a problem for Peython and Kareena. Now it was time for the waldoes to march.

Blade signaled to one of the Kaldakans he had selected to control the main console. The man was handling it well, switching frequencies from the scout waldoes to the combat ones. Then Blade looked to the left and to the right, to make sure Bairam and Sidas were in their chairs and that everyone else was out of the way as they were supposed to be. Then he signaled again to the man controlling the console. That would be the last movement he'd be able to make for quite a while without a couple of dozen waldoes imitating it.

The controller switched on the three chairs, and Blade stood up. So did Bairam and Sidas. Forty miles away, so did ninety combat waldoes, thirty responding to each chair. Blade flexed all his limbs, cut in the vision and sound circuits, and saw waldoes all around him doing the same thing. It was grotesque, like ninety gigantic metal puppets all doing gymnastics in unison.

Blade and his comrades bent down and gripped wooden rods. Ninety waldoes also bent down and picked up metal bars four feet long and three inches thick. They had no grenades, but they would still be well-equipped for close combat.

Blade saw one of the waldoes fall over, heard Bairam curse, and sighed. Peython's son was so excited that Blade would have rather had someone else in the third chair, but there *wasn't* anyone else.

"All right," said Blade. His voice came out distorted by the helmet and the controls in his mouth. "Waldoes—forward *march*!"

And they marched. Eighty-nine waldoes tramped forward, crushing down the bushes which had screened them, and stumbling down the low slope behind. They weren't in good order to begin with and it got worse as they moved, because they were moving at three different paces. They all did move, and by the time they reached level ground they were moving fast.

Thirty miles an hour, Blade calculated, was the waldoes' top speed. They were five miles from the valley. Ten minutes' marching. That should give the Doimari plenty of time to put their heads into the trap, without giving them time to spring one on the Kaldakans.

"Waldoes—right *face*!" shouted Blade. He felt more like a drill sergeant than a commanding officer. "And test your clubs."

Eighty-nine right arms swung eighty-nine metal bars. The arm jammed on one of Sidas's waldoes, smoking and sizzling. Sidas had the wisdom not to make the waldo drop its club. Otherwise all his waldoes would have dropped theirs and had to pick them up again. Bairam's waldoes swung their clubs more wildly than the other men's. Blade heard clangs and crashes as clubs struck other waldoes and hoped Bairam's enthusiasm wasn't doing any damage.

"Forward—*march*!" again, and the waldoes started off. They jammed together for a nerve-wracking minute at the narrowest part of the path between the hills. Blade froze his waldoes in place and let the other two men sort theirs out. Then the waldoes set off. The ground shook under their feet as nearly three hundred tons of metal accelerated. Dust rose in a fog, and the clanking and squealing of long-unused joints and cables was as loud as the sounds of a battle.

Most of Bairam's waldoes rapidly pulled ahead, then some began to drop back, joints smoking. The boy was pushing them too fast. When Blade saw two of them literally trip over their own feet and fall, he'd had enough.

"Bairam! Get out of that chair and stand back. You'll wreck half your waldoes before the battle starts, the way your're going!"

Bairam looked both rebellious and ready to burst into tears. Then the controller moved quickly in obedience to Blade's hand signal, cutting off the power to Bairam's chair, after switching its frequency to Blade's. Without blinking or missing a step, Blade took over Bairam's waldoes. Bairam muttered a few comments on the sex habits of Blade's parents, then stamped off to join the spectators.

Halfway to the battlefield now. The smoke from the burning forest was beginning to spread across the landscape. Blade could now hear the sounds of the battle ahead over the din of the waldoes themselves. It was impossible to tell who was doing what to whom, but no mortars were firing. That probably meant the Doimari were doing what he wanted them to do—move across the valley after the Kaldakan advance guard. They'd also have to go around the forest, but that wouldn't spoil Blade's plans.

Then Sidas's chair suddenly began giving off smoke and sparks. The controller seemed to leap halfway across the room to cut its power, then drag Sidas clear. He was rubbing scorched spots on his arms and legs but otherwise seemed unhurt as he ran toward the next activated chair. Reluctantly Blade froze all the waldoes in position. He didn't want to take the risk of controlling all of them single-handed, not when battle was so close.

As Sidas ran, Bairam snatched up a bucket of water and emptied it over his comrade. It was just as well for Bairam that Blade could do nothing but curse at this helpful gesture. Throwing water around near a shorted-out chair could have knocked out the whole command center and lost the battle in a second! But there was no time to explain electricity, and probably not much point in explaining it to Bairam at all. At this moment Blade would have promised his right arm to bring the waldoes a mile closer to the battlefield.

Then Sidas was in his new chair and controlling his waldoes again. A few had fallen when Blade stopped them, but only one stayed down. Eighty-six left now, and only minutes to the battlefield. The smoke was getting so thick

169

that Blade wondered if it would interfere with lasers. It was certainly getting thick enough to interfere with his vision.

The last bend into the valley was the sharpest, and getting all the waldoes around it was the hardest job yet. They had to slow down almost to a walk, to make sure that a dozen waldoes didn't go down on rough patches of ground. For a minute the waldoes would have been a magnificent mortar target, and Blade found his palms sweating. The smoke he'd feared now came to his rescue. It swirled back and forth across the valley, completely blocking the view of the Doimari.

The Kaldakan waldoes were almost ready to move again when the first Doimari infantry drifted out of the smoke. They were only a straggling line of scouts, but that was enough for Blade.

"Sidas! Your lasers!" he shouted, and bit down on the firing button for his own weapons. In his excitement he'd forgotten to turn all of his waldoes directly toward the Doimari, and most of the beams shot wide. That did no harm. The Doimari were too frozen with surprise and fear to react in time. On the second volley, more than fifty laser beams struck the scouts. Blade saw a few smoking bodies fly into the air, but most simply vanished as if they'd been vaporized. Probably some of them were. The rest must have been buried under the mass of smoking earth thrown into the air. From behind the smoke came the screams of men on the edge of the destruction, not too badly burned to cry out.

The smoke wasn't going to affect the lasers as much as Blade feared. Very well, then let the butchery start. He'd known all along there'd be a gory spectacle but in the first excitement of seeing the enemy at hand he'd forgotten it. Now he remembered, his hands and mouth were dry, and he had to swallow before he could give his next order to Sidas.

"All right, Sidas. Face yours forward, and fire on my command."

"Yes, Blade."

He sounded subdued. Blade hoped he was. He distrusted

bloodlust in other people almost as much as he distrusted it
in himself.

Blade bit down on the firing button, saw the laser beams
lance the smoke ahead, and heard the screams.

"Fire!" More of the same, then:

"Waldoes of Kaldak, *charge*!"

Chapter 23

Rehna tried to peer through the smoke from the burning
forest on the north side of the valley. She wanted to see
how the battle was going.

For the moment at least it hardly deserved the name of a
battle. The only Kaldakans in sight were the handful of
dead they'd left behind on the north slopes. Rehna didn't
know if they'd been driven off completely or just driven
back to another position. Certainly they were now out of
range of either the Doimari infantry in the valley or the
Fighting Machines on the hills to the south.

For the moment the Fighting Machines were staying
where they were. Those were Nungor's orders, Rehna had
passed them back to the Seekers in the control chairs in
Doimar, and so far they seemed to be obeying. Rehna did
not like Nungor or trust many of his captains, but she
knew that if each part of Doimar's army fought its own
battle the Kaldakans might still win.

Some of the Doimari foot soldiers were going north and
some south to get around the fire and renew the attack.
Others were going nowhere, either too busy licking their
wounds or because they hadn't received any orders. Rehna
saw Nungor run past several times, more red-faced and

sweating harder each time, shouting orders, trying to get the lazy ones moving. She wished him luck. For now her own part in the battle was so easy that she had time to realize she was hungry. That wasn't surprising, since she hadn't eaten all day.

She bent over and started to call down the hatch. Then she heard a sudden swelling uproar from the smoke to the west. Screams, the sound of lasers, and a metallic chorus which sounded like Fighting Machines on the move but couldn't possibly be that.

Then in a moment Rehna knew that the impossible was the truth. A line of Fighting Machines loomed out of the smoke, all marching the same way regardless of the ground underfoot, all swinging blood-stained metal bars in their hands, all with fire-beam tubes glowing like evil eyes in their chests. Behind the first line was a second, behind the second line a third—

No! Logic, sanity, and common sense all shouted that in her mind. She ignored the shout, because her eyes told her differently. The Kaldakans had live Fighting Machines, and they were coming down the valley against the men of Doimar like Death itself.

Then the Fighting Machines stopped, and the first row shot their fire-beams. Hundreds of Doimari were already running or lying down, but that didn't save most of them. The fire-beams made a net like a fisherman's in the smoky air, and the Doimari foot soldiers were the fish. Some flew completely into the air, trailing smoke. Others fell, writhing and screaming, their clothes on fire. Still others became puffs of greasy smoke or were torn into bloody rags when the fire-beams set off their hand fire-bombs.

Some men lived a bit longer, because the beams didn't catch them or because the smoke and dirt thrown up weakened the beams. Many of these died in the next minute, when the Fighting Machines strode forward, swinging their clubs. Rehna was reminded of farmers beating their fields for blue rats. One blow of the steel clubs the Fighting Machines carried could turn a man into pulp from his head down to his chest.

The Fighting Machines swung clumsily and all together, whether they had a target or not. Rehna saw one smash the

172

arm of the machine next to it with its club. It looked as if a few men or perhaps only one man was controlling all the Fighting Machines at once. That was something she knew was possible but which Doimar had never tried. If there was one man controlling all the Kaldakan machines, she though she knew his name.

Blade of England.

Suddenly she wasn't quite sure she wanted to bear the child of a man who'd slaughtered so many of her fellow Doimari. However, she was sure he wasn't going to win the battle, in spite of the bloody start he'd made. When the Fighting Machines of Doimar came down into the valley, each one would have a trained Seeker controlling it. Blade's crude tactics and skills could never meet such an attack.

While she'd been thinking this, the Kaldakans moved a hundred paces forward and used their fire-beams again. This time she felt the heat on her face and clods of earth rattled off the armor of the Carrying Machines. She looked anxiously at the Voice equipment, but it seemed unhurt. They'd still better move back to a safer position.

A breeze seemed to be carrying the smoke away now. To the north Rehna saw Kaldakan foot soldiers appearing on the ridge again. To the south she could now make out eight or ten of Doimar's Fighting Machines. Any moment now they should start down the hill, to pass through the retreating Doimari foot soldiers and engage the Kaldakans. The battle would be hard and would destroy much Oltec, but it would also prove, even to Nungor, that the Seekers—

"No!" This time Rehna said the word out loud. Then she screamed it at the top of her lungs, as if screaming loud enough could change what she saw. The Fighting Machines weren't coming down the hill. They were turning away into the smoke and walking off the battlefield. No, not walking—they were starting to *run*. Rehna's fellow Seekers were more concerned with saving their Fighting Machines than saving their fellow Doimari, or even winning the battle.

"No," Rehna said again, and burst into tears. "No!" she shouted, pounding her fists on the armor of the Carrying Machine until she tore open skin and flesh. She went on pounding, as blood made the armor slick under her. "Cowards! Cowards! Cow—"

Fire-bombs exploded all around her, and something like the metal fist of a Fighting Machine struck her. She flew through the air and landed hard enough to knock the breath out of herself: More explosions crashed out as the Carrying Machine started moving off. The Voice equipment was now leaning drunkenly to one side. She hoped it still lived.

Rehna knew what was happening. The fire-bomb throwers were shooting at the Kaldakan Fighting Machines, but they didn't know the exact range. They were landing their bombs short, right among the Doimari! "No," she whimpered.

Then more explosions, and a rain of metal pieces, human bodies, and broken weapons fell all around her. She tasted blood in her throat, gagged on it, and also felt a pain deep in her belly. Was she losing the child?

A single fire-beam stabbed through the smoke overhead, from a Kaldakan machine controlled by someone as good as any Seeker. With horrible precision it sought out the Carrying Machine with the Voice equipment. The Voice equipment sagged and started to melt, someone on fire from head to foot jumped out, then the fire-boxes inside gave up all their energy at once. The explosion rolled Rehna over on her side, so she didn't see the red-hot wreckage of the Seekers' proudest achievement. She did see a Kaldakan Machine bring down one foot within inches of her face, the other on top of a Doimari soldier who was mercifully already dead. She didn't see any more clearly, because the pain suddenly struck her all over so that she curled up into a little ball and started whimpering.

"Mother, mother," she said, as the Kaldakan Fighting Machines marched past her.

By the time Kareena brought the Hovercraft and her father down into the valley, the slaughter was over. There were no living Doimari in the valley, or at least no living Doimari it wouldn't be a mercy to kill. The Kaldakan infantry spread out and began to finish the victory the waldoes began.

174

To Kareena, there was an even worse sight than the Doimari bodies. Over half the Kaldakan waldoes stood or sprawled useless, their power exhausted, joints frozen or broken, weapons burnt out, killed by lucky grenade or rifle shots from desperate Doimari at short range. Kareena felt sick at the sight of so much ruined Oltec, and even Peython was confused.

"Did Blade destroy the waldoes deliberately, I wonder?"

"He would not do that, Father."

"I still wonder. Perhaps he wanted to destroy them, so we would not grow weak or evil from the strength of our Oltec as Doimar did."

Kareena had no reply to that, and concentrated on steering the Hovercraft through the scattered Kaldakan soldiers. Then she saw something familiar about the body lying on its side fifty paces ahead. A moment later she recognized the bloody face. It was Rehna, the Seeker woman who'd shared Blade's bed the night of the escape from Kaldak.

Kareena stopped the Hovercraft and leaped out before her father could question her. She knelt by Rehna and looked down into the pain-glazed eyes.

"Mother . . ."

"The Lords of the Law be merciful, Rehna." She drew her knife and thrust quickly, surely home between Rehna's ribs. When the woman slumped in peaceful death, Kareena pulled the hood of her robe over her face, then stood up and started cleaning the knife.

As she finished, a waldo loomed out of the smoke. She jumped and nearly screamed out loud. The waldo bent at the knees and started tracing a message in the dirt with the tip of a twisted, blood-spattered club.

KAREENA. GIVE NEW POWER CELLS TO THIS WALDO. I MUST GO AFTER DOIMARI WALDOES. TRUST SIDAS. THANKS FOR MERCY TO REHNA. BLADE.

Then the waldo sat down, and the hatch on its back which covered the power cells sprang open. Kareena stared for a moment, then turned and promptly collided with her father.

"Look where you're going, Kareena."

"I'm sorry, Father. I—I'm not as calm as I ought to be."

Peython looked around at the valley of death now ap-

175

pearing out of the thinning smoke. "No. None of us can be."

While the Kaldakans repaired his chosen waldo, Blade climbed out of the control chair and relaxed as much as he could. The last stage of the battle would be as demanding as running a marathon, and it would be almost entirely his job.

The Seekers' panicking and withdrawing the waldoes had cost Doimar the battle and probably opened an irreparable breach between the infantry and the Seekers. It would also save the waldoes to fight another day if no one chased and destroyed as many of them as possible. That was a job for a single waldo with plenty of power, controlled by the best waldo operator in Kaldak, which meant Blade. He'd smashed the Doimari infantry by using the massed waldoes like a battering ram. Now he was going to finish the day by using a single waldo like a rapier.

Blade drank some water and listened to the conversation among the technicians. He heard someone mutter, "Why did Kareena give that Seeker bitch a good death?" He was about to turn on the man himself when he heard Bairam's reply.

"Because she deserved one," he said coldly. "She fought and died as a brave warrior, though she fought with Oltec as her weapons. Do not say anything against her in my hearing, or Kareena's."

"Yes, Bairam."

Blade grinned, Bairam was still an odd mixture of man and boy, and it was almost impossible to tell from one hour to the next which one ruled him. If Peython lived long enough, though, Blade knew a man would succeed him as chief of Kaldak. Geyrna would help, too, although it would be a while before she had much thought for anything except her grief over her father's death. There was another man who'd died like a warrior even though he was not one, and indeed had even less duty on the battlefield than Rehna.

Then it was time for Blade to man the control chair again. The technician and Bairam strapped him in, then turned to Sidas while Blade tested his waldo. If anything

176

went wrong with Blade's chair, Sidas would take over with his until Blade could make a quick shift.

Everything in the waldo worked, including the laser. Blade discarded the old, battered club and picked up a new one. Then he took a deep breath and put the waldo into movement, on the trail of the last of Doimar's army.

When the Fighting Machines marched away, the foot soldiers of Doimar—Nungor's pride—fled in panic like munfans from greathawks. For an hour or more Nungor tried to rally them, appealing to their courage, their honor, even their hatred of the Seekers. They were deaf to anything except their fear of Blade's raging Fighting Machines, and after a while they started cursing their War Captain. A little while longer, and some of them were firing shots at him. Nungor gave up trying to rally his army and started thinking of saving Feragga. He told himself that he wanted to save her because with her alive the war could still be won even after the lost battle. He knew some might doubt this, but he did not really care what they thought if he could only get Feragga away from this butchery.

Now he and Feragga were trotting over the hills a good two hours' march east of the battlefield. The air around them was clean, and only a few human stragglers were visible. A dozen or so Fighting Machines were also in sight, some walking steadily, others lurching or sometimes falling down. Some of the Seekers were skilled enough to keep their Fighting Machines moving even after the Voice Machine was dead. But what use was that sort of skill, if they had no courage, no loyalty to their comrades? Apparently the Seekers never asked themselves that question. Well, they would pay for that and everything else they'd done wrong today, even if Feragga cast him out of his office and her bed for it!

Then far off to the west Nungor heard the ugly sound of a heavy fire-beam in action. It came a second time, then the prolonged hissing of a Fighting Machine exploding. Feragga looked at him.

"Are those damned Seekers fighting among themselves now?" she asked, in a voice which hinted she was for once ready to believe almost anything about the Seekers.

"Probably a machine breaking down," said Nungor. "Or maybe some Kaldakans are catching up with—" He stopped as they both saw the same thing in the same moment. A Fighting Machine of Kaldak, striding over the hills like a giant walking among dwarfs. In one hand it swung a metal club, like a boy walking through a field and knocking the heads off thistles with a stick. Its head swiveled, the fire-beam stabbed out of its chest, and the arm of one of Doimar's machines flew into the air. The crippled machine turned to face its enemy, and took the second fire-beam squarely in its chest. It fell over backward, and a third beam tore through its lightly protected crotch so that everything inside it vanished in blue flame and billowing smoke.

"Blade!" said Feragga and Nungor together. Feragga continued to stare at the approaching machine, while Nungor ran toward the nearest Doimari machine. He shouted as he ran.

"Seeker! Seeker! You damned coward, bring that piece of iron over here and pick up Feragga! Pick up your lady and run her to safety! Pick her up, or, by the Lords, I'll burn every Seeker alive when I get home!" As he said this he realized that his chances of ever getting home were rapidly vanishing, but as long as Feragga's remained good—

Nungor was about to give up hope, when the Fighting Machine turned toward him, then tramped past and bent over Feragga. She shouted in surprise and fear as the metal hands picked her up, then shouted again as she saw Nungor turning back toward Blade's machine.

"Nungor, damn you! You can't—"

"Yes, I can, my lady and my love. Your safety is Doimar's future. My life will not be much loss if it ends here." He shouted for the Seeker to hear. "Now get that scrapheap moving, and get your lady out of here!"

Dirt flew as the Fighting Machine's feet dug in. Then it was on its way, walking, trotting, finally running, with Feragga clinging desperately to its head and straddling one shoulder. She still looked back as long as she could.

After the machine started running, Nungor didn't pay it any more attention. He lay down behind a fallen Fighting Machine, and put three fire-bombs and a fresh fire-box ready to hand. Then he aimed his rifle at the towering

178

figure of Blade's Fighting Machine and waited for it to come into range.

Blade's waldo was moving at a walk because Blade himself needed to catch his breath. He'd come nearly ten miles, most of it at a run, and on the way destroyed eighteen Doimari waldoes. Only four had given him any sort of a fight. Destroying the rest was like shooting fish in a barrel.

Then in the distance he caught sight of a waldo running off with a human figure perched on one shoulder. He increased the magnification of the visual scanners and recognized Feragga. Suddenly he found he had the strength to run again. He wasn't going to be able to catch most of the waldoes, but if he could catch Feragga and kill or capture her—Well, she was all that held the balance between the Seekers and the infantry. Take her out of the picture and there'd be civil war in Doimar. Kaldak would have a complete victory without losing another soldier or firing another laser blast.

Blade was starting to run when the laser hit the waldo in the head. It didn't wipe out the visual scanners, but it dazzled him so that it was a moment before he could see clearly again. When he could, he saw Nungor crouched behind a fallen waldo, his rifle aimed for another shot.

Blade started turning the waldo's own laser toward Nungor at the same moment the War Captain fired again. This time one scanner died, and Blade felt a sharp pain in his head. That was odd—damage to the waldo didn't register as pain in the operator. The controls had automatic cutouts—

The pain in his head grew sharper, and suddenly Blade knew what was happening. The computer was calling him back to Home Dimension—now, of all times!

"Damn!" Then he shouted, "Sidas—get ready to take over. I'm going to be sick."

Sidas nodded, the technicians switched on his chair, and all its wiring promptly went up in a cloud of smoke. Sidas screamed and through pain-blurred eyes Blade saw the technicians beating out little fires all around him. They pulled him out of the chair, though, and from the way he was swearing he didn't seem to be seriously hurt.

179

"Bairam—get into a chair and take over. Now, for the Lord's sake and Kaldak's future. Move, you stupid little—!"

Those were Blade's last words in Kaldak's Dimension. He knew he shouldn't have called Bairam "stupid," tried to apologize, but found the pain in his head freezing his jaws. Bairam dashed past and leaped into the first chair he reached, shouting to the technicians, "Quick! Blade's after Nungor and Feragga! If we can kill them—"

Then Blade couldn't hear any better than he could talk. He fought desperately to hold onto sensation in this Dimension as long as he could, but the battle was as hopeless as ever. He felt as if his head was being wrenched apart, then the command center vanished and in the next moment the computer room in the Project complex took its place. He'd made the transition between the Dimensions almost between one breath and the next.

Then Blade realized he was still in the control chair, not in the KALI capsule, and it was teetering drunkenly. He tried to straighten up, but his transition-slowed reflexes weren't fast enough. The chair went over with a clanging crash which echoed around the room. Blade felt new pains all over, the sharpest one in his jaw. He saw J's face bending over him, twisted with alarm. Then he stopped seeing faces or feeling pain as a comfortable, soothing blackness took him.

Chapter 24

"Good night, Mr. Blade."

The blond nurse sounded disgustingly cheerful. Blade wouldn't have replied even if his broken jaw hadn't been wired shut so that all he could do was grunt. She went out, and Blade was alone in his hospital room, waiting for the sleeping injection to take effect.

He'd been tempted to refuse it, but that would simply have brought the doctor back in to make a fuss, and Blade was in no mood to be fussed at when he could only grunt in reply. At least Lord Leighton and J hadn't insisted on his doing more than writing a brief summary of his adventures this trip, although he suspected the scientist would do his share of fussing as soon as Blade could talk again.

Perhaps it was just as well that Blade wouldn't be talking for about ten days. He was in a thoroughly vile temper over being snatched back to Home Dimension when there was so much left undone in Kaldak and so many questions he'd never have answered. Did Bairam kill Nungor and catch up with Feragga? What happened between Kaldak and Doimar after that? How was Kareena doing with his child? Was she considering Sidas as a possible husband, as he'd hinted she ought to?

Blade made a string of noises which with an unwired jaw would have been a string of oaths. He *would* keep his temper when he could talk again, and tell Lord Leighton and J everything they needed to know and everything they asked in addition. He would even help the Project's scientists test the control chair—apparently they were excited about something in it, although he didn't know exactly what. Lord Leighton hadn't been able to explain it in plain English.

After that, though, he was going to say good-bye to the Project and everyone else who knew him from Adam for at least two weeks. He'd go on a walking tour and perhaps look for a country house he could buy cheaply. He had been looking for country property for sometime, since in his London apartment he couldn't keep Lorma, the hunting cat he'd brought home from the Forest of Binaark on his last trip. She deserved better than a cage in the Project's complex even if he did visit her every few days to see that she was well fed. He would tell Lord Leighton what to do with the Project for those two weeks, and if the scientist protested he would head for Brazil and try a career as chief of a tribe of Amazon Indians! Enough was enough.

In spite of his irritation, the sleeping injection was beginning to work. Blade leaned back on the pillows and let it do so. By the time the nurse came back, he was so soundly asleep that even her knocking over the bedpan and having to clean it up didn't make him blink.

In Kaldak, the people from the command center sat at the entrance, breathing the night air and listening to the sounds of their city celebrating victory. None of them wanted to stay down below and have to look at the empty space where Blade and his chair had been.

"He must have been one of the Sky Masters themselves," said Bairam to Sidas. "They sent him to bring us out of the darkness, then took him home when his work was finished."

"I don't know that it was finished," said Sidas. "But certainly the rest is up to us." He thought of Kareena.

Peython and Kareena sat beside a fire, watching steaks cut from a captured munfan broil over the fire. Peython held his daughter as he had when she was a little girl. Kareena rested her head against her father's chest and thought of another meal of munfan steaks, with the father of her child who had now gone—far away, she knew that much.

Twenty miles away, Feragga of Doimar sat staring into another campfire, waiting for Nungor. She knew now that Doimar had lost and would have to make peace once and for all with the triumphant Kaldakans. She had been betrayed by Blade, and that hurt her deeply. Ah well, at least she still had Nungor.

But Nungor lay on the hilltop behind the fallen Fighting Machine, half his head burned away.